Perfecto Mundo – a novel b⸗   ᴜ May 2007

Carl and Mandy Rutherford's cruise around the Gree.   ⸗urns into a nightmare as strange natural phenomena strike the earth whilst they ᴀ.   ⸗uba diving off the island of Spetse. As the days pass it becomes clear to them that they could be the only people alive in this part of Greece, perhaps in the whole of the Mediterranean or even worse.................

As they venture further afield looking for other survivors and an explanation to what has happened whilst they were diving, things fall into place and the awful realisation of the truth dawns on them and the people they team up with.

An epic adventure and a tale of the strength and resilience of the human race as the survivors of the greatest natural disaster to have struck the earth in millions of years battle for survival and to repopulate the planet – perhaps with a little divine intervention?!

CHAPTER ONE

The sun was a bright yellow orb just rising behind the ancient, whitewashed buildings of the beautiful Mediterranean island of Spetse. At the heart of the Aegean, this small, quiet island is a Mecca for tourists from all over the world who want to 'get away from it'. The streets were deserted and there was a peaceful, lazy silence, which was normal as the only modes of transport permitted on Spetse are bicycle, foot and horse-drawn carriage. No traffic pollution, noise or snarl ups here. Out in the small bay of Vrelos Beach a small yacht bobbed lazily on the slight swell of the clear blue water, its ensign flapping in the slight breeze indicating that the owners were of British origin.

In the small aft double cabin of the yacht, Carl Rutherford raised his head from the pillow and glanced across at the bright green luminous display on the laptop screensaver clock. 08:27 it announced to the world in vivid, lurid flashing green that did little to alleviate the dull throb he'd awoken with in his temples.
"Shouldn't have started on the ouzo last night", he thought to himself as he cast his eyes around the small, compact cabin of his new retirement toy – a Moody 38 cruising yacht, purchased with his recent windfall from the sale of his business – located his shorts, pulled them on and climbed onto the deck.

The clear blue sky sported not one single cloud to blot out the bright, golden sun, which already had enough heat in it to make Carl think of taking a quick swim instead of a shower. He popped back down the varnished wooden steps into the small galley and lit the gas stove. Filling the bright copper kettle from a bottle of spring water, he shouted through to the aft cabin "wake up sleepy head – it's half eight on a beautiful Mediterranean retirement morning". He put the kettle on the gas hob. "Get up and make a brew will you love? I'm just going in for a dip", shouted Carl as he climbed the steps back up on deck, shrugged off his shorts and dived naked into the cool, turquoise waters, making a huge, frothy white splash as he entered with his legs flapping wildly behind him.

Back on board the yacht, stirring lazily and stretching deliciously under a tumble of sun bleached blond hair; Mandy rubbed the sleep from her slightly bloodshot blue, round eyes and groaned slightly. She too had overdone it on the ouzo the previous evening and her furry tongue and slightly thick head were the price she now had to pay. It had been worth it though. The locals in the Taverna in Vrelos had made them feel very welcome last night and the Meze they had enjoyed was one of the best yet on this trip. She and Carl had dined on calamari, olives, warm pitta bread, hummus, taramosalata, tahini, thick chunky pork kebabs, small pieces of Kleftiki lamb, god knows how many carafes of the local house red wine and, of course, the inevitable ouzo.

They had been in the Mediterranean for only a few days now at the start of their adventure since selling the business, having sailed the new yacht themselves all the way from the UK, across the Bay of Biscay, through the Straits of Gibraltar and following the warm sun Southeast across the Med towards the Aegean. It had been an uneventful five week trip with no bad weather, good winds and fantastic July and August sunshine nearly all the way. They were in high spirits and feeling very good about life – and why shouldn't they be? They had both worked hard all their lives building up a business which they had now sold and were reaping the rewards.

In the past they had experimented with sailing and flying, both having passed their 'Day Skippers' and 'Yacht Masters' courses over many years spent holidaying on the south coast. They had also both passed their Private Pilots License only last year after a couple of years worth of lessons and classroom work. However, the draw of the ocean and the fact that they both took more naturally to the sailing rather than the flying led them towards a 'life on the ocean wave' rather than a retirement spent clogging the airways. To be truthful Mandy had struggled a lot with the navigation side of flying but took to it like a 'duck to water' on the sailing side of things.

Although they had kept their small, stone built cottage just outside Morpeth in Northumberland, they had vowed to each other that they would try and spend at least six months every year on the yacht sailing wherever the fancy took them. This first year they had both decided on Greece and were in the process of trying to find a suitable port in which to moor the yacht and where they could call a home away from home for at least this summer. So far they had done most of the Aegean – perhaps they would try the Ionian next and maybe next year around the Croatian coast. Who knows? Who cares?

Mandy rose naked from the double bunk, allowed herself one final lingering stretch as she stared at herself in the full length mirror attached to the back of the cabin door. "Not bad girl" she said aloud to herself. She was already well tanned from sunbathing on deck throughout the journey and her body was becoming toned from the hard work put in on the ropes and sails when the wind was good enough for them to make way under sail rather than with the motor. "Not bad for 38.....not bad at all", she said to herself as she wrapped a large fluffy beach towel around herself and walked through into the galley where the whistle at the end of the kettle was just starting to proclaim that the water was boiled.

She made two cups of black, decaffeinated coffee, no sugar (part of their commitment to a new and healthier lifestyle whilst aboard – which went totally to pot last night!) and carried them up the steps onto the deck. She looked out over the large shiny chrome steering wheel and instrument panel of the boat and spotted Carl floating lazily on his back in the water just a few metres from the rear ladder of the boat.
"There's a cup of coffee here for you. Come and get it" she shouted to him. He turned and waved an acknowledgement to her and started the few lazy strokes required to get him back to the ladder where he pulled himself up and into the yacht with ease. For such a big man he moved with amazing agility and Mandy was amazed at how a man who had spent many of his working hours in quite a sedentary role could have such a well toned body. At 6' 2", 45 years old and already very darkly tanned Carl was not the atypical 'Geordie' stereotype. Usually blondish, ruddy faced descendants of the Vikings that invaded the Northumberland shorelines centuries ago, most Geordies still to this day had features reminiscent of those ancient ancestors and Mandy was a typical example of this, with her long blond tresses and deep blue eyes.

"Do you think the name suits her – have we chosen well" Carl asked Mandy as he accepted the thick, plastic mug of steaming black coffee from her. The yacht was named after the Norwegian goddess of Summer and the daughter of Odin, 'Gretchen', which was also the name of Carl's mother who had passed away only last year and had been the inspiration and driving force behind the sale of the business and the early retirement. "Life's too short to spend most of it working" she had instructed them, "believe me I know".

"She's solid, well built and reliable as well as a thing of beauty" said Mandy "I think the name is just perfect. Anyway, how's your head this morning. I feel a bit thick headed but I'm still up for that dive if you are".
"Of course" replied Carl. "It'll take more than a few carafes of wine and a few ouzos to put me off my stride. We'll have a bite to eat then motor over to the lagoon around the south side of the island. I'll check the diving gear, you rustle up some breakfast".
"Okay", replied Mandy dipping back down the steps into the small galley. "Bacon butties do?" she shouted up.
"Perfect" shouted Carl in reply. "Brown sauce on mine please and another cup of coffee".

Carl opened the fibreglass side lockers to the port side of the steering wheel that housed the diving gear and started pulling out the masks, snorkels, weight belts, demand valves and air tanks that they would need for their dive later that morning. They wouldn't need wetsuits as it would only be a shallow dive and the water temperature was at the warmest it was going to get this summer already. Both tanks gauges read 'full' as he had topped them up yesterday from the onboard compressor that he had ordered from the yacht manufacturer as an 'added extra'. They had both been keen divers for many years and had heard of the wreck of a German World War 2 fighter plane purported to have gone down in the bay of Hermetes at the southern tip of the island. The plane is a shallow water dive, is apparently very well preserved and draws hundreds of divers to the Blue Lagoon every year.

The smell of grilling bacon wafted up the galley steps onto the warm morning air and Carl finished checking the tank gauges and went down below. Over bacon sandwiches and fresh coffee they discussed their plans for the dive and what they would do for lunch and for the rest of the day. They decided on a homemade lunch onboard but would need to go ashore after the dive and buy some supplies from the one of the small grocers' shops in Hermetes.
"Tuna, some salad stuff, crusty bread and a few cold beers" said Carl "what do you think".
"Perfect replied Mandy", clearing away the dishes and washing them quickly in the tiny galley sink. "Let's get this show on the road then" she said shrugging off the beach towel and putting on her one piece, coral blue swimsuit. "You up-anchor and start the motor and I'll stow everything away down here. It's not worth sailing around to it – it's only a mile or so" said Mandy, disappearing into the cabin to pull the bedclothes straight and put away clothes and shoes from last night.

Carl started the engine with the small silver key in the instrument console and left it to idle and warm up while he hoisted the anchor. He could see the small Taverna on the quayside where they had spent last night and a small gaggle of children and dogs playing outside it with a stick and a rubber ball. The children heard the engine start up and waved to Carl. Carl waved back, finished stowing the anchor and headed back to the steering wheel where he slipped 'Gretchen' into gear and turned her hard to starboard into the open sea heading south towards the Blue Lagoon. Mandy finished her tidying up and came up from below and stood beside him as he steered the boat away from Vrelos. She put her arm around him, gave him a kiss on the cheek and said "I'm so happy we decided to do this".
"Me too. Mum was right – life is too short to spend most of it working. I just wish she was here with us now to enjoy this" said Carl as he spread his arm out in a gesture taking in everything that lay ahead of them.

CHAPTER TWO

'Gretchen' pulled smoothly into the small bay at Hermetes and Carl put her in 'bows to' on the small jetty. They moored her up and both stepped ashore and strode up the jetty towards the tiny village square, where already the local old men, gnarled from years of hot sun and toil on the fishing boats were sipping their strong black coffee and playing drafts and chess in the shade of the parasols.
In the grocer's shop they bought what they needed for the day, ordered two coffees at the local bar next door to the grocers and went and sat on a small bench underneath a large drooping mimosa tree in the square.
"Are the underwater GPS units fully charged?" asked Mandy. They had invested in two wrist watch type Global Positioning Systems for underwater use. These would tell them their positions to within a couple of feet and would ensure that on any dive, they could

always find their way back to the yacht however far they had swum away from it during the course of their dive. These clever pieces of technology worked on signals received from satellites positioned hundreds of miles above the Earth's surface similar to a SatNav system used in many of today's cars.

"Yep, they're fully charged and working as they should. The wreck is only 8 or 9 metres deep so we can spend a good while down there too. Finished your coffee?" They both drained their coffee and headed back to the jetty.

Out in the middle of Hermetes Bay, with a little bit of scouting around, the wreck was clearly visible from the surface through the fantastically clear water. They could see hundreds of small black fish swimming lazily over it and silhouetted over the almost white covering of sand that surrounded the wreck. Once anchored and happy with the stability of the yacht, they donned their diving gear, did their final checks and tumbled backwards over the rear swim platform into the warm Aegean waters. Although the water was warm it still took Mandy's breath away as she entered the water and her nipples stood out proudly against the wet material of her swimsuit. Carl gave her an approving look; they both made the International diving sign for OK with thumb and forefinger in a circle and descended to the wreck in a swirl of bubbles.

Once settled on the bottom they both quickly adjusted their kit and when they were both comfortable they once again gave each other the OK and set off to explore the wreck and the myriad of wildlife that surrounded it.

The plane was in amazing condition and although most of the exterior was covered by sheen of plankton and barnacles the German Iron Cross decals on the tail fin and wings could still be clearly seen. In the cockpit most of the instrument panel was still visible and underneath the wings they could make out the bulbous shapes of what could either be some kind of missile or fuel storage tanks.

Carl checked his depth gauge and found that they were at 8 metres which meant they could stay down as long as their air reserves allowed them and would not need to worry about decompression stops when ascending.

He checked the GPS system and his tank air gauge and all was fine when suddenly he was almost blinded by the brightest light he'd ever seen. Like an explosion of a million luminous flares the whole ocean around both of them seemed to erupt into a phosphorescent sea of light. The blinding light was all encompassing, as if the ocean were on fire and they both closed their eyes against it to protect them but even through the closed lids Mandy could still see the brightness and she could feel an intense flash of heat which lasted only for 3 or 4 seconds and then faded away shortly followed by the dimming of the intense light.

Inside their facemasks they both dared to gradually open their eyes and, although the light had gone they both had dark spots in their field of vision that would take several minutes to clear, similar to when a person looks into a light bulb for a few seconds then looks away and blinks but can still see the outline shape of the bulb.

Carl caught Mandy's eye and gave the thumb up sign indicating that they should ascend to the surface. She acknowledged with an OK sign and they both started to rise slowly to the surface. As they surfaced Carl checked his GPS to ascertain how far they were from the yacht. The screen of the small gadget was completely blank. He tapped it a couple of times but with no result.

As their heads popped through the surface of the water, Carl removed his mask and swivelled around with the use of his fins and breathed a sigh of relief as he spotted 'Gretchen' only a hundred metres or so away from them bobbing listlessly on the slow swell.

"What the hell was that?" shouted Mandy across to him once she too had removed her mask. "It nearly blinded me".

"I don't know" replied Carl "let's get back to the yacht and see if we can find out. It looked like it could have been an explosion of some kind but I didn't hear a noise or feel any vibration – just the light and......did you feel some heat as well for a few seconds?" he asked her.

"Yeah, I felt that too" replied Mandy.

Once up on deck and fully de-kitted they both went down below to towel dry and then sat facing each other across the small table in the main galley area.

"What do you think it was then?" asked Mandy.

"I don't know" replied Carl. "Plane exploding overhead......gas explosion on shore.....I don't know, there was no noise, no reverberation through the water, only the light and the heat, and now it looks as though nothing ever happened. Everything seems normal up here. The GPS stopped working though. I wonder if it had anything to do with that."

"Maybe" said Mandy, "I'll put the radio on and see if there's an English channel. Maybe there'll be something about it on the news. How about a spot of lunch? Tuna salad, crusty bread and an ice cold beer".

"Sounds good to me", said Carl. "I'll just put the dive gear away while you get it ready".

Carl went up on deck in his trunks and started to put the dive gear back into the storage bins. As he worked he had a strange feeling; an eeriness came over him and he felt uncomfortable. Something wasn't quite right and he couldn't put his finger on it. He looked around at the landscape and took in the beautiful turquoise waters gradually darkening to a deep blue as they receded towards the horizon. He looked in the other direction and saw the small port of Hermetes about half a mile away where they had bought their provisions earlier on.

"What is it? What is it that doesn't feel right?" he asked himself. He listened to the gentle breeze knocking the rigging gently into the mast and thought to himself that if it picked up a bit they might get some good sailing in this afternoon, perhaps head over to Piraeus and have a couple of days of comparative luxury in a hotel in Athens before carrying on to wherever the whim took them.

Then, it came to him. Apart from the rigging clattering away on the breeze, there wasn't a single sound to be heard. He looked over towards the small village jetty and cocked his head away from the breeze and listened intently.

Nothing – no children playing, no barking dogs, no seabirds calling – nothing except the breeze and the gentle tinkling of the rigging.

"Mandy", he yelled, "Come up here quickly". Mandy climbed the steps from the galley. She had had changed from her damp swimsuit into a pair of tight fitting white shorts and a baggy T-shirt proclaiming that she was 'With Stupid'.
"Wassup?" she asked.
"Listen" said Carl. "Listen carefully and tell me what you hear" he said.
Mandy stood behind the large chrome steering wheel on deck and cocked her head the same as Carl had done. She listened intently for a few seconds and said "I don't know what you're on about. I can't hear a thing" she said.
"Exactly – that's exactly it. There isn't a sound coming from the village, there are no seabirds. I can't even see anyone on shore in the village, no kids playing, nothing. Was there anything on the radio?" he asked.
"It was dead" she said, "Only static wherever I tuned it to".
"Something isn't quite right", said Carl. "Do you fancy motoring over to the village to see if the locals know anything or if there's anything on the TV in the bar about that flash of light?"
"Okay", said Mandy, "but lunch is ready so let's have that first, then we'll go over. I need some tampons anyway. My period's overdue by a couple of days now and I don't want to be stranded somewhere remote without a shop and not have any when the time comes".

They erected the small temporary table to the rear of the instrument panel on deck and sat down to lunch. The sun was high in the sky now and very warm and they discussed the possibility of starting out towards Piraeus later on, what type of hotel they should get – budget or luxury – what type of meal they would prefer. Mandy opted for Chinese and Carl said he would go with that but would have preferred a steak. They agreed to decide as they walked around scoping out the restaurants later and, as they finished their lunch and started to clear away the dishes and the table both had a quiet inner feeling of unease that neither of them could put a finger on.

Finished with the clearing up, Carl weighed the anchor and Mandy started the engine and steered 'Gretchen' back in towards the small harbour of Hermetes. As the village came closer and closer Carl looked out for any signs of noise or movement on shore. There was nothing – absolute silence and no movement of any kind.
"Very strange" he thought, but said nothing to Mandy as they moored once again, bows to, against the small jetty and tied off the yacht.

CHAPTER THREE

Carl had also pulled on a pair of shorts and a similar baggy T-shirt to Mandy's, this one announcing 'Me Too' indicating that he also was 'With Stupid' and together they stepped off the yacht and strolled hand in hand up the jetty towards the village square. Normally they would pass a few wizened old fishermen, sat in the shade of their small quayside huts, mending fishing nets, smoking and chattering among themselves. There would be the odd dog and cat, sniffing around the quayside for scraps of food or old fish heads, a tasty morsel to snatch and secret away to enjoy later.
Nothing, no-one. No children playing on the rusty old swings on the parched earth of the village square, no old ladies dressed in black walking with their shopping baskets to and

from the small village square. No old men with a small opaque glass of ouzo topped with ice and a thick black espresso sat at the outside tables of the village bar, no clatter of drafts or chess pieces – nothing.

"Where is everyone?" asked Mandy. Carl looked at her, shrugged his shoulders and said "let's try in the shop again".

They walked over to the village shop, parted the bright plastic beaded curtain that was erected to keep out the flies and emerged into the cool, dark interior of the shop. The scent of ripe watermelons, freshly picked bulbs of garlic and hundreds of other smells greeted them and Mandy shouted out, "Hello…..Yassou…..anyone here?"
The dark interior of the shop was empty. Towards the back of the shop was a narrow doorway leading to the living accommodation. Carl walked to the rear and popped his head through the doorway and shouted "Yassou, Hello – anyone at home?"
No response. Carl turned and looked at Mandy, shrugged and gave her a look that said 'what the hell?' and went through the door into the living quarters. Mandy followed him into what must have been the family living room. The room was sparsely furnished with bamboo and wicker furniture and lots of green potted plants covered almost every available surface; Clothes were strewn all over the floor and furniture and a small colour portable TV flickered away in one corner of the room, picking up nothing but static. The blinds were down to keep out the fierce afternoon sun and the room was dark and quite cool. "Yassou, hello" shouted Carl one more time.

"Come on Carl, let's go" said Mandy. "There's obviously no-one here and I feel a bit awkward being in someone else's living room uninvited. Let's try the rest of the village."

They stepped back out through the beaded curtain onto the small narrow street and shielded their eyes against the bright sun. "Let's split up and look for people then meet back here in a few minutes" suggested Mandy.
"Okay", agreed Carl. "I'll go that way" he said indicating a clockwise direction around the village via the bar and the Taverna, and you go that way. We'll meet back here in a few minutes. Yell out if you find anyone" he said.
"Okey Dokey" replied Mandy and off they went their separate ways, each occasionally shouting "Yassou" and "Hello" and popping into small buildings, houses and huts in the hope of bumping into one of the locals. "Perhaps they're all having a village meeting" thought Mandy to herself as she systematically searched her way through the village. "Or maybe they're all in church. What day is it?" she asked herself. Try as she might, she couldn't remember what day it was. "Retirement and sailing around the Med willy nilly has that effect on you I suppose" she thought to herself but she thought she would check out the church further up the small hill heading inland – just in case it was a Sunday or some religious festival or public holiday that they weren't aware of.

Meanwhile, on his search through the opposite end of the village, Carl was having no luck locating a living soul. He opened people's front doors, shouted, went in and moved on down the street repeating the process with no luck. The silence was eerie. Not even the steady chirp of the cicadas which, oddly enough you didn't hear until suddenly, they were no longer there to hear.

He headed back to the square after about 15 minutes searching and got there just as Mandy also returned. "Any luck?" he asked her.

"Not a soul" she replied "in fact, strangely enough, not even a cat, dog, chicken, goat, sheep….nothing at all. Where is everyone Carl? It's a bit spooky".

Carl thought for a few seconds and said "look, I bet it's some kind of festival day in another village and everyone's gone over there for the day. Perhaps that bright flare up of light that we saw was just some monstrous firework display. You know what the Greeks are like for their fireworks".

"Perhaps" she agreed, not convinced. "So shall we sail around somewhere else and take a look then?" she asked.

They headed back through the hot afternoon air buffeted from the brilliantly whitewashed walls of the fishermen's' huts along the jetty and boarded the yacht. They cast off and headed north around the island with the intention of staying close to shore and pulling into the first marina, bay or harbour where they could see signs of life. As they travelled by motor, all thoughts of hoisting the sails forgotten for the moment, they passed scores of small bays and marinas with no sign of life when suddenly Mandy shouted out above the dull throbbing note of the engine, "look Carl, over there – another yacht".

She pointed off shore and sure enough, less than half a mile from them was another yacht, seemingly stationary with its sails flapping all sloppily in the wind, like sheets hung out to dry and forgotten.

Carl adjusted course with the large, chrome steering wheel and headed towards it. As they approached, Mandy headed up to the bow near fore anchor and began shouting "Hello, Hello – anyone there?" There was no sign of life so Mandy threw a couple of tethered fenders over the port rail and Carl pulled alongside with his port side to the starboard side of the new yacht.

Still yelling greetings, Mandy stepped over the guard rails of both boats and went down below into the cabin of the other yacht. Carl watched on and she re-surfaced onto the deck about 20 seconds later. "No-one here" she exclaimed with an extremely puzzled look on her face. "The way the sails are set it looks like they were just sailing along and then just left everything as it was and disappeared or jumped ship or…….whatever, I don't know" she said to Carl.

She was looking quite distressed so Carl said to her, "come back over here babe and I'll take down the sails and anchor it up then we can report it to the Greek Coastguard as soon as we find somewhere with some life". They swapped places, Carl did what he had to do on the other yacht and they set off once again.

"I think we should just head for the mainland towards Piraeus" said Carl. We're bound to pass loads of yachts, ships, Blue Dolphins and we can see what's going on".

"Okay" replied Mandy, and off they set heading North in towards the busy shipping port of Piraeus just to the west of Athens.

They both tried their mobile phones on several occasions to try and contact friends and relatives, but despite being able to access full signals from the local service providers like Athena Telecom and Hellenic Telecom, they were unable to obtain a single ring tone to any country they dialled.

En-route they did indeed see many yachts and other boats but not one of them appeared to be manned. In fact they even saw some that were motoring along with no-one at the helm and as they pulled into the normally bustling port waters they even saw a few larger boats that had collided with each other. But nowhere did they see any sign of life at all, human or otherwise. As they pulled up to an empty berth on a floating decked marina within the port authority, they said little to each other and looked very apprehensive as the disembarked and proceeded on foot to explore the, now silent, deserted ghost town that was once the bustling port of Piraeus.

CHAPTER FOUR

Except, it wasn't quite silent was it? There was, in the distance the low hum of background noise that you would get in a town. "What is that noise?" thought Carl. They could hear no hustle and bustle, no evidence of human noise – chitter chatter, vendors in the nearby markets plying their wares, shouting from the docks – none of that. Carl thought to himself that the noise they could hear was traffic noise in the far distance.

They walked hand in hand, all senses on heightened alert away from the docks and marina jetties and towards the exit to the Port Authority. The heat had almost gone out of the sun now and Carl checked his watch. Almost 6pm. "Let's see if we can grab a cab or a bus into Athens. We can always find a nice hotel and pop back later for some fresh clothes and our toiletries" he said to Mandy.

She agreed and they walked across the still hot, black tarmac surface of the Port Authority concourse and out onto the main coast road that runs from Piraeus into Athens, through the heavily built up and populated seafront areas.
As the emerged through the grand ornate gates into the street they were met by a scene of carnage. The noise had suddenly increased and now they could see why. There was the mother of all traffic jams with cars literally nose to tail in both directions of the single carriageway road. Nose to tail was correct, because almost every car was touching the one in front of it and with some of them; the damage caused indicated that they had collided at a fair speed.
Almost all of the car engines were still running but, although Carl and Mandy looked up and down both carriageways into every vehicle they couldn't see a single driver or passenger.
"Carl, there are clothes and watches and wallets in all the cars I'm looking at over here" shouted Mandy.
"Same over here" shouted Carl, "it's as if the people have just disappeared. Look over on the pavements as well".
Mandy looked over at the pavement area that ran along in front of the shops and buildings facing the port. Scattered everywhere were an assortment of clothes and

personal items that looked as though they had just been shrugged off by their owners and left on the street where they dropped.

Greek Bouzouki music blared out of one of the doorways over to the right of them heading into Athens. They both walked over to what appeared to be a small bar and restaurant. There were seven or eight bar stools pulled up to the bar, each with a pile of clothes draped over and around them, and on the floor an assortment of loose cash, wallets and watches. In front of each bar stool, on the bar were a selection of drinks and half finished plates of food.

Carl and Mandy looked at each other, mouths hanging open in incredulity and Carl, trying to lighten the atmosphere, shrugged and said with a forced laugh "maybe Scotty has beamed them all up".

Mandy just looked at him, wide eyed, her face a seeming pale with fear and a look of bewilderment and replied, in all seriousness "do you think it could be something like that, really?"

"Of course not", said Carl. "I was only joking. But obviously something has happened and I reckon that it has something to do with that flash of light".

"Well why has everyone else disappeared and we're still here, walking around as if nothing has happened?" Mandy asked him.

"Well, I know this sounds a bit unlikely but maybe it's because we were underwater at the time of whatever it was that occurred" offered Carl as his suggestion.

"I think you're right" said Mandy "and if that's the case then there will be other people about too. Swimmers, divers, oil rig workers and submarine crews......well you know, anyone else who might have been underwater at the time...." she trailed off weakly.

"Look" said Carl "let's get ourselves along the coast towards Athens and as we pass the beaches we're bound to see someone who was swimming at the time".

They headed east along the blocked carriageway, the noise from the car engines diminishing little by little as they walked because some vehicles reached the limit of their fuel reserves and had spluttered begrudgingly to a silent death.

They'd been walking about 15 minutes and had left the built up area pretty much behind them. They were now on a stretch of beachfront road with the beach to their right and in the distance to their left the sprawling suburbs of the outskirts of Athens.

On the beaches, which had obviously been busy earlier on, were parasols, towels, cooler bags, swimming costumes, beach balls – in fact everything associated with a good day out at the beach – apart from the people. Not a soul.

"What about your swimming theory now then Carl?" asked Mandy. "Surely some of these people must have been swimming when that flash came?"

"I know, I know" he replied, furrowing his brow as he thought. "Maybe they weren't deep enough under the water. What if you had to be a certain depth to be protected from whatever it is that's caused this?" he speculated. "Don't forget we were a good eight or nine metres deep. That could have made all the difference".

Mandy thought about this for a few seconds then her face beamed. "So let's find a dive shop or a dive school then. Someone else must have been diving off the coast somewhere at the same time as we were" she offered.

"Okay" said Carl. "Look – over there. There's a scooter. Let's grab that and head further along". He pointed to a fairly new, bright purple Vespa laid on its side on the edge of the curb. Hoping that it had only stalled and not run out of fuel, Carl hit the starter button and the machine fired into life at the first touch.

They both hopped on and Carl headed slowly east, dodging the melee of stalled and idling vehicles, sometimes riding on the pavement, sometimes on the road and they gradually came into areas of denser housing and even more snarled up traffic. Still no people though.

"This is it" Carl turned around in his seat and said to Mandy. "This is more or less the city centre. There's the Acropolis over there and look – over there – a hotel. Let's go and check it out".

They pulled over off the main drag and parked the scooter behind two black Mercedes right outside the entrance to the Inter-Continental 5-star hotel and walked in to the plush, air-conditioned and discreetly lit interior of the lobby.

"At least the power's still on" noted Mandy as she walked over to the check in desk, where, waiting to check them in was a full set of receptionist clothing strewn about the chair and floor behind the check in desk.

"Look, it's getting late" announced Carl. The sun was just setting outside over the distant tops of the columns of the Acropolis and the light was fading fast. "I suggest that we take advantage of the fact that we appear to have a 5-star hotel all to ourselves and rest up here for the night. Tomorrow we can search the city and the beachfront areas of anyone that might have been diving or doing anything that helped them survive whatever it was".

"Miners" offered Mandy.

"What?" said Carl.

"Miners" she repeated "or anyone in a tunnel or underground for whatever reason. Surely they would have been as protected as us underwater?"

"Good thinking, we'll start searching tomorrow" said Carl. "Meanwhile, let's find the best room in this place and then raid the kitchen and the bar, not necessarily in that order".

CHAPTER FIVE

They walked behind the reception area to where the keys were kept. This was a traditional hotel. No electronic cards to swipe at the bedroom door in this hotel– these were real keys on chunky brass key fobs that seemed to weigh a ton and would ensure that the bearer did not go home with the key 'accidentally' in their pocket.

They selected the key labelled 'Honeymoon Suite', hoping that because the key was still on the rack that the room had previously not been occupied.

Carl walked over to one of the three elevator doors and pressed the amber 'up arrow'. The faint whir of the elevator descending from a higher floor seemed to trigger something in Mandy and she turned towards Carl and said "Carl, I think we should use the stairs. What if the power goes off while we're going up in the lift? It's bound to go off sooner or later if there are no people around to man the power stations".

"Oh my god. I never thought of that" replied Carl. "That could have been disastrous. Possibly the only two people left alive in the world and we die of starvation or suffocation in a lift stuck between floors. We're going to have to be on the ball and think about what we're doing in future" said Carl as he turned towards the stairs.

"Luckily the honeymoon suite is only on the second floor" said Mandy as they climbed the elegant, slowly spiralling, marble staircase together.

They let themselves into Room 202, with the brass plaque on the door assuring them that they had indeed found 'The Honeymoon Suite'. The bed was made and there was no sign that anyone had been in the room since it was last serviced by the maids. Two fluffy, white bathrobes were laid out at the foot of the bed each with a hand wrapped chocolate truffle resting on the top. Mandy opened one of the truffles, popped in into her mouth and said to Carl "this is lovely and I've just realised how hungry I am".
Carl agreed saying that he too was starving. He was in the bathroom and shouted through "Mandy, it's got a Jacuzzi. Why don't you run it and I'll go and get us a bottle of wine or champagne or something? We can have a soak, then go and explore the kitchen and find something to eat".
Carl left the room and headed back down the stairway while Mandy turned on the elaborate gold plated mixer taps on the Jacuzzi and started to strip off her T-shirt and shorts. She poured some of the complimentary bubble bath into the warm flow of the water and watched the surface foam up with rich, coconut smelling suds that looked so inviting.
As the water filled, she stepped into it and slowly laid back and closed her eyes. Her hand reached out to the control pad on the side of the Jacuzzi and pressed the 'ON' button. The surface of the water erupted into a seething mass of bubbles and the rich aroma of tropical coconut seemed to increase and fill her senses. Above the low whirr of the water pumps Mandy heard the clinking of glasses from the bedroom and a few seconds later a totally naked Carl stepped through the bathroom door carrying a tray holding two champagne flutes and an ice bucket revealing the gold foil, already popped bottle of something distinctly Champagne looking.
"Dom Perignon" announced Carl. "Hundred quid a bottle in the UK. Would madam like a glass?" he asked.
"Madam certainly would" replied Mandy as Carl poured two glasses and handed one to Mandy as he lowered himself into the opposite end of the huge tub and sighed with pleasure.
"Apart from it possibly being the end of the world as we know it, I'm having such a nice time" he said, taking a sip of the exquisite champagne. "What about you" he asked.
I'm frightened Carl" replied Mandy. "I mean, what if we can't find anyone and we really are the only people left?"
"Impossible" speculated Carl. "There has to be other people all over the world just like us who are wandering around now thinking the same things as us. We've just got to find them – and we'll start tomorrow. Tonight let's just chill out and get a good night's rest - after we've raided the kitchens".

They finished their first glass of champagne while they soaked leisurely in the Jacuzzi and, after towelling dry and donning the lovely, soft, fluffy bathrobes set off down the stairs in search of the kitchen. They found it through some double swing doors leading off from the aptly named 'Acropolis' restaurant. This room was very grant with stucco walls adorned with huge hand-painted pillars and ancient Greek figures in brilliant white togas. They entered the kitchen and scoured the huge banks of matt silver catering fridges and freezers and the rows and rows of pantries. They put together a huge tray of sliced meats and pickles, cheeses and crusty bread. Mandy found some butter, cutlery and napkins on a service table just inside the waitresses' door and, laden with a full tray, they made their way back to the reception area and the start of the staircase that would take them back up their room.

On the way back up to the bedroom with their little tray of culinary treasures, feeling a bit like naughty schoolchildren 'post-theft', Carl said "let's just check out the phones and Internet while we're here at reception".
They placed the tray on the reception desk, went through to the back office and Carl sat himself down in the black leather reclining office chair pulled up to a plush mahogany desk and clicked on the Internet Explorer icon on the screen of the office PC.
Meanwhile Mandy was busy on the telephone. "I'm going to try e few of our friends and family in the UK whose numbers I can remember off the top of my head" she announced. "Don't forget to dial 00 44 first" replied Carl, "I'm just seeing if the web's working".

They both bashed away at their respective keyboards studiously for a few minutes. Carl eventually broke the silence by announcing hat the Internet was working fine, which meant that the power must still be on in the areas that supplied the main servers.
Mandy announced that the phones appeared to be working fine. She'd phoned a few friends in the UK, got the ring tone fine but no answer from anyone. This was strange as it was evening in UK and people should be in either watching TV or tucked up in bed.
Carl also commented on how, even though the Internet was working none of his contacts were showing as online either on MSN Messenger or Yahoo Messenger.

Each harbouring their own thoughts, they collected their tray of food and made their way back up the staircase to the Honeymoon Suite. They ate their fill, finished off the bottle of champagne and just before they decided to go to bed for the night Mandy turned on the TV to station after station of static. Carl opened the hotel window and looked out over the bright twinkling lights of what should have been a busy city nightlife. The lights were on all over the city but the only noise came from the few remaining engines that were still being supplied with fuel. Carl was sure that all of these would have died out by morning and that they would wake up to silence.

CHAPTER SIX

They both slept fitfully that evening and when the sun's rays started filtering in through the heavily brocaded drapes and dappling the room in bright dancing patterns, Carl got straight out of bed and drew them open. He looked out of the window which they had left open in the night in case they heard any sign of life – perhaps a vehicle passing by, or someone shouting out, searching for other people.
They heard nothing and now, of course all engines had ground to a halt on the streets below and there was absolute silence. Over to his right Carl could see the broad blue expanse of the Mediterranean Sea stretching away to the distant light blue of the morning horizon. There wasn't a single boat to be seen, not a single person to be seen, not a

seabird (or any other bird for that matter) to be heard and Carl turned to Mandy and said "right, what's our plan of attack then?"

She sat up in bed, hair tousled, suntanned skin dark against the clean, white crisp cotton bed linen and replied "you can't seriously expect me to come up with a plan to save the world until you've made me a cup of coffee……can you" she teased.

Carl filled up and plugged in the kettle on the complimentary beverages tray and while it boiled he showered and pulled on the same clothes as he had worn the previous evening. He then made two cups of black, de-caffeinated coffee, thinking "posh hotel – they have de-caff", while Mandy also showered and dressed.

As they sipped the coffee and tore into a packet of complimentary oatcake biscuits they discussed what they should do that day. Mandy was in favour of going back to the marina, picking out a large, fast motor cruiser and start exploring all around the coast until they found some other people.

Carl was of the opinion that they should make their way out to the airport because possible other people may do the same and there was always the chance that they could commandeer a small aeroplane. As he pointed out, "we can cover a lot more ground if we search from the air and we can go wherever we like".

They agreed on Carl's plan. Carl had always been the dominant force in any decision making throughout their 14 year marriage whether it was a new car, what type of yacht, even family panning strangely enough.

Carl had wanted children from the start of their marriage. He argued that the veterinary business could easily support them if Mandy had to give up work. She agreed reluctantly at first but gradually came around to the idea and they spent many happy months 'practising'. However, the months started to turn into years and eventually they sort medical advice because Mandy just was not conceiving.

They underwent every medical fertility test available in the UK and after many months the specialists were baffled. They were both perfectly healthy and there was absolutely no reason why Mandy could not conceive. Carl's sperm count was high, in fact above average and Mandy's 'plumbing' as one gynaecologist referred to it, was in perfect working order. They were told to persevere and that it would just be a matter of allowing enough time to allow other Nature to do her job.

After 14 years though, both had become accustomed to the idea that it just wasn't going to happen and that had been a major deciding factor in the purchase of the yacht and the early retirement.

They emerged from the hotel at 7.30 am, the morning sun already warm over to the east of them and promising a hot Mediterranean summer day ahead. They decided to try and find a large, powerful 4 x 4 all terrain vehicle for their journey out to the airport which was, as Mandy read dutifully from a brochure she had picked up as they left the hotel lobby *"located between the towns of Markopoulo, Koropi, Spata and Loutsa, about 20 km to the east of central Athens (30 km by road, due to intervening hills). The airport is named after Elefthérios Venizélos, the prominent Cretan political figure and Prime Minister of Greece, who had an outstanding contribution in the Cretan rising against the Ottoman occupation of Crete in 1896".*

"At least we know which towns to look out for on the signposts then. Mind you, it should be well signposted even from the city centre" pointed out Carl. As they walked along a street full of shops and restaurants searching the abandoned traffic for a suitable vehicle Mandy suggested that they get a few supplies together in some of the deserted shops, some of which still had music playing in the background, doors wide open to attract something that possibly they would never have again – customers. Carl agreed and they searched out a large hypermarket, grabbed a wheel around shopping trolley and embarked on a bit of a mini supermarket dash. They grabbed a few tinned and dried goods, chocolate and crisps, bottled water and both stripped naked at the clothing section, ditched their own clothes and fitted themselves out in a completely new outfit each. Carl also grabbed a medium size rucksack into which they crammed their goodies and the headed out of the store. As they headed past the toiletries department Mandy said "oh wait a sec" and grabbed a box of tampons from the shelf. " I'm a couple of days late" she explained" and, when Carl turned away she also picked up a ClearBlu pregnancy test kit and shoved it into her pocket as they left the store and resumed the search for a suitable vehicle.

About 50 metres up the street from the hypermarket they spotted the perfect solution – a Silver Toyota Landcruiser. This could be good because it wasn't stuck in the traffic but was parked outside a small 'gyros' take-away kebab shop. Could it be their lucky day? Indeed it could because on closer inspection Carl noted that the key was in the ignition. It had full cream leather interior, air conditioning, SatNav, 4-wheel drive option, in fact this baby looked as if had every available option Toyota could throw at it – and just to make life easy. Question is – how much fuel did it have? Did the owner - whose shorts, underpants, shirt and sandals still adourned the driver's side along with his watch and wallet – leave the engine running while he popped in for his kebab or had he turned off the engine? Carl checked the key. It was in the off position. He turned it and the 4.0 litre diesel engine roared into life and settled down to a steady, healthy sounding idle and Carl checked the fuel gauge which was showing three quarters full.

"Perfecto Mundo" shouted Carl to Mandy "in you get madam, your carriage awaits". To get the Toyota out of its parking space they had to manouevre onto the pavement and drive a while on the pavement, which was just wide enough, until there was a gap in the nose to tail traffic just by a set of traffic lights. Strangely enough the traffic lights were still working which was more than could be said for the car's SatNav system Carl noticed. "Looks like we'll need to keep an eye out for signposts Mandy" he said "the SatNav isn't working".

As they started to weave their way through the traffic heading away from the coast looking for a signpost to wards the airport, the stationery traffic thinned out and made the driving a lot easier although in several palces they had to manouvre by way of the pavement, central carriageways and grass verges. They drove for about a mile heading in a general direction away from the coast and the buildings became less commercial and more residential until eventually they broke away from the outskirts of the city. The road here turned into dual carriageway and they spotted a blue tourist sign for the airport. The stalled and crashed vehicles were now appearing only sporadically, although when they did see crashed vehicles the damage seemed to be far more severe, probably due to the faster speeds they had been travelling at when the 'event' occurred.

They passed the outskirts of the small towns of Pallini and Kantza, saying little between themselves, each one closely observing their side of the road looking for signs of life. With a sign to the airport informing them they had 8km still to travel, Carl spotted a thin plume of black smoke straight ahead of them in the direction of a small village named Spata according to the road signs. Carl pointed the smoke out to Mandy and they agreed that they should turn off at the junction to Spata and go and investigate the source of the smoke which was spiralling lazily upwards in the warm haze of the early morning, sun warmed air. At the start of the village outskirts they rounded a slow curving left hand bend, the view obscured by rows of pretty whitewashed villas with lush green gardens sporting orange and lemon trees and pretty purple Jacarandas. Mandy wound down her window to smell the fantastic citrus and floral fragrances on the breeze and as they came out of the corner into the heart of the village her mouth and eyes were agape in awe at the scen that greeted them.

Carl slowed the Toyota to a smooth halt as he too looked in up astonishment at a huge blue and white, Olympic Airlines jumbo jet that now blocked their passage. The plane had demolished most of the small village as it had furrowed a shallow, almost canal like, trough about 500 metres long across farmland, through houses, businesses and gardens before coming to a stop here on the edge of the village. The huge towering cockpit above them glinted from the sun and just behind the cockpit was a wide, shard edged crack in the metalwork which broke the plane into two halves. Both wings of the plane were missing but apart from that, strangely enough, the plane hadn't suffered too much damage and the black smoke that was issueing forth was coming from the rend in the metalwork which Carl guessed was at the galley area of the upper deck.

"Fuel, what about the fuel?" shouted Mandy "it's not caught fire yet. Let's get the hell out of here before the fuel catches fire".
"Relax…..can you smell fuel"? asked Carl. "The wings are missing. They must have come off further back earlier in the crash. I can't smell fuel because, I think, the fuel tanks are built in to the wings. This must have been coming in to land when IT happened".

"This could be happening all over the world – planes crashing, traffic pile ups, train crashes, ships chugging along with no crew….." Mandy stated as if suddenly the awful truth was just dawning on her. "What about when the power stations go off, what about gas lines, what will we eat – there's no animals……Carl?".

"Relax – calm down – everything will be fine" Carl said with steady re-assurance. We'll find other people, we'll find food and there are generators and fuel and vehicles and all sorts of resources out there that are just ours for the taking so we're going to be fine. What's more – it's all free" he finished, trying to lighten the mood and lift Mandy's spirits.

They climbed back into the Toyota, turned around and set off back to the route to the airport. After a few minutes back on the dual carriageway they exited at the airport slip road. The runways looked clear, although there was an Easyjet plane stuck in a tangled heap in the fencing at the end of one runway which they assumed must have been taxi-ing or taking off when the light struck. They pulled up at the front of the airport terminal building, weaving in and out of the stalled traffic, mainly taxis. Near the double doors at the entrance to Departures was a large white mini-bus with the engine still running. "That's strange" thought Carl, "that engine should have died long ago". He got out of the Toyota and went across to the mini-van. His heart leapt as he approached and saw the Sky blue lettering on the side of the van indicating that it belonged to The Hellenic Dive and Snorkel School. "Mandy, look at this" he shouted as she climbed from the vehicle. She came over to the side of the mini-bus and her face lit up. "There must be someone inside" she said and she turned and entered the double doors, which were still operating on mains power, followed by Carl. They heard immediately the sound of people talking in the otherwise cavernous silence of the huge departures lounge. They looked around and up on the first floor on the café concourse sat around a table drinking cups of tea or coffee was a group of 4 people, two men and two women who looked like they were in their mid-twenties. The group spotted Mandy and Carl at the same time as they spotted the group and averyone shouted simultaneously "Hello". The word echoed around the vast emptiness of the lounge like a sonar sounding device and Mandy had to suppress a nervous giggle of relief. They'd finally found some other people, real people! Mandy couldn't belive it. She really thought they might be the only people feft in the world. She silently chided herself now, as they climbed the stairs to the café, for being so silly.

As they approached the table the four people got to their feet and there was a general hubub of excitement and chatter as everyone introduced themselves and all talked over each other in their rush to tell their stories and find out what each other knew. The four people consisted of two couples, all best mates living and working in London.

It turned out that Mike and Hannah lived in Ealing and ran a small pub in the Firkin group 'The Lettuce, Slug and Firkin'. Mike was a strapping lad about 6' 3" with huge broad shoulders and biceps stretching the flimsy fabric of his FCUK T-shirt, that looked like they'd been nurtured on a regular basis in a gym. There wouldn't be much trouble in their pub and God help anyone who tried to touch Hannah while Mike was around. She was a very pretty, petite strawberry blond with the cutest turned up pixie nose and beautifully even, pearly white teeth Carl had ever seen. Carl thought to himself that he had never seen anyone that looked less like a pub landlady in his life.

The other couple, Tom and Lucy, as well as being best friends with the other two, were also their best customers at the pub. Tom was a short, stocky fellow with deeply tanned skin, almost Mediterranean looking, althought his cockney accent gave away his true roots. He was a policeman in the Metropolitan Police Force and Lucy, his fiancee was a nurse. The four had met whilst on a diving course in the UK 4 years ago and were still firm friends to this day. Lucy, like Hannah was also petite with a typical English Rose complexion and almost black hair. She had the kind of skin that went pink, then red, then peeled then went pink again.

The six of them made themselves fresh cups of coffee in the café servery and sat back down at the table. Carl told his and Mandy's story so far to the group and when he had finished Mike took over the narrative for their group.

They had been under instruction with the Greek guy that ran the small dive company, The Hellenic Dive and Snorkel School. His name was Costas and that day the five of them were in a small shallow bay around the coast at a place called Drapestona. They were doing an exercise in about 5 – 6 metres of water which involved dropping all of their kit, fastened together, to the seabed. Tank, demand valve, weight belt, mask, snorkel and flippers. The idea was, Mike informed them that they each had to swim down to the kit, put on the mask, find the mouthpiece of the demand valve, then in a set sequence, (weight belt first so that they didn't start to rise prematurely back to the surface) put the rest of the kit on so that they were fully kitted out. They had all four descended to their respecive kit and were at varying stages of putting it on when they saw the same light that Carl and Mandy had seen. Mike had actually been looking up towards the surface at the time to where Costas was treading water and watching their progress wearing only mask and snorkel. Mike was blinded for a second or two after the flash of light and when he got his sight back there was no sign of Costas, only his trunks, mask and snorkel drifting slowly towards the bottom of the bay. At this point they had all abandoned any attempt at donning their kit and come back to the surface almost as one.

They'd climbed back into the small inflatable dive boat that they'd anchored near the dive site and started talking among themselves trying to fathom out what had happened. After that, their story was pretty similar to Carl and Mandy's. They'd got their heads down for the night back at their apartments after hours of fruitlessly searching for people, animals anything and trying telephones and Internet. They'd decided to come to the airport on the off chance that other survivors might do the same thing – a hunch that now, obviously, had paid off.

Tom now took over with the speculation "So I reckon it was some kind of radiation or strange frequency we've never encountered before put out by something like…. I don't know….. a solar flare maybe, or something to do with all the satellites or an asteroid crash….. something like that. I'm not buying the idea of aliens 'beaming everyone up'. I did a bit of looking around on the Internet and there were quite a few references to Gamma Rays being the next big threat. Apparently, the ozone layer used to protect us from them. Nobody knows what effects they would have on living beings and if there was some kind of deep space explosion or something, perhaps Gamma Rays could have broken through the ozone layer…..or maybe even some other kind of rays that we don't even know about, What do you guys think?"

"It's got to be somethng along those lines" agreed Carl "something that obviously can't penetrate a certain thickness of water, as your mate Costas found out. We need to know if it also didn't affect anyone that was underground below a certain depth at the same time as well. That way there's going to be a lot more survivors".

"That's the worrying thing" Lucy chirped up. "How do you mean, worrying?" asked Tom. "Well" repled Lucy "let's just say that the only people left in the world were either underground or underwater at the time of the.... whatever it was.....phenomena. Well, they're probably going to be mostly men. Miners, submariners, divers. I mean, there will be women too, tourists diving or visiting tourist attractions like caves and caverns or whatever but it will be mostly men".

"And that's worrying you because.....?" asked Carl. "Well", she said."eventually those men are going to want women, and with women in short supply I just think there's going to be a lot of problems....serious problems, even life threatening problems. I just think we should think very carefully before we decide what steps we should take next, that's all" she concluded. There was a short silence as all six of them pondered what Lucy had said.

"Don't worry Luce" chirped up Tom in an attempt to lighten the atmosphere a bit, I'll protect you kid". Carl believed he could as well. The Metropolitan Police were after all one of the best trained Police Forces in the world and Tom, although short and stocky, looked like he could handle himself. The mood lightened a bit and a lively debate ensued about what they should do next. Mike got a round of sandwiches and crisps from the café counter for everyone as they talked. He commented on the fact that the sandwiches were one day out of date but who could complain when they were free. In fact, it suddenly dawned on him that from now on, everything was going to be free. Then, without warning the lights throughout the whole airport concourse suddenly went out. The low background hum of electrical machinery petered out and there was a still, eerie silence. The local power station had finally given up the ghost.

CHAPTER SEVEN

The silence and the now gloomy light of the concourse seemed to spur the six into action. A quick debate followed and it was agreed that they would search for a plane that Carl and Mandy felt they could comfortably fly and that would accomodate all six of them. They would then do a fly-over of Athens and the surrounding areas looking out for any signs of life. They set off as a group towards the hangars at the east end of the airport away from the terminal buildings where they could see a small armada of privately owned planes of all shapes and sizes parked up in neat orderly rows. They were a deceptive distance away and the hot, still air bounced up from the shimmering black surface of the tarmac and made the walk a hot and sweaty affair.

When they eventually reached the area where all the private planes were lined up in almost military precision, they wandered, as a group, up and down each aisle looking at the various machines on offer. "What about this one" piped up Tom "it looks really cool and it looks like it will seat all of us no problem. It's huge in fact. Must be 10 or 12 seats in there".

Carl replied, "It also has two jet engines and is made by Lear. Way out of our class I'm afraid. We're looking for a single engine propellor driven plane, preferably a Cessna of some kind because that's what we were trained on". As he finished talking he turned the corner and started up a new aisle and stopped in his tracks as he looked at the first plane in the aisle. "Mandy – I don't believe it – look a Cessna Stationair. Come and have a look" he shouted. All of them came dashing around to Carl and stared at the sleek lines of the pure white, almost brand new looking aeroplane and Hannah asked if this one was okay. Carl and Mandy pointed out the six leather seats inside the spacious cockpit and the fact thatit was a single engined Cessna. Not the exact model they had learnt in, which was a much smaller model called the Skyhawk but with very similar instrumentation and handling.

They all vied for position, trying to look through the small aircraft portholes, shielding the glare from the sun with their hands, at the plush leather interior. Mike tried the doors on both sides and announced that they were locked. "Not to worry" said Carl " the keys will be hanging up in the office in the hangar over there. Come on". They all headed over to the huge corrugated metal hngar on the edge of the airfield which, as well as housing even more small planes, did indeed have a small office stuffed away in one corner. The office was open and in the small metal key locker fixed to the wall they found the keys with a bright yellow plastig fob announcing CESSNA STAIONAIR – SX ARG. Carl explained that SX ARG was the registration mark of the aeroplane and SX identified it as a Greek plane. As they walked back to the Cessna he also explained what he could remember about this plane. "It will cruise for between four and a half and six hours at 6500 feet and is capable of about 280 kilometres per hour but we will be flying lower and slower looking out for things. Let's hope the tank is full" he said.

Luck was on their side because the tank was indeed full and that wasn't the only surprise. As well as the full cream leather interior it was also fitted with air conditioning. As they all settled into their seats and Carl and Mandy started on the pre-flight checks, the other four 'oohed' and 'aahed' at the array of buttons, dials, gauges and gadgets in the spacious cockpit of the plane. "Costs about half a million dollars US brand new this baby" said Mandy "so it should have every gadget on it. As Carl started the engine and the air conditioning started to kick in, Mandy pointed out to the other four the individual headsets with attached microphone for each of them. She showed them how to operate the headsets and as she turned around back into her co-pilot seat and donned her headset, Carl began the short taxi to the end of the runway, which was completely clear apart from the Easyjet plane still silently entangled in the wire fencing at the far end.

As they accelerated down the runway and Carl lifted the small plane gracefully into the air an onlooker would be forgiven for not realising that this was happening amidst probably the greatest natural (or otherwise) disaster that had befallen the planet, probly since the demise of the dinosaurs. The atmosphere in the small, plush interior was that of a group of friends setting off at the start of their holidays however once they'd reached a height with which Carl was happy they all settled down to the task of looking out down below for any signs of life.

"I'm just going to fly at about 2000ft and keep going out in ever increasing circles for a couple of hours. If we haven't seen anything by that time we'll head back to the airport.

I'm doing things visually because the Satellite guidance systems aren't working" Carl announced to everyone through the headsets. He thought to himself – 'just like the Toyota, just like the diving SatNav. Whatever it was must have destroyed the satellites or made them inoperable as well'.

As they circled, creeping ever outward from the central starting point of Athens they flew at times over the mainland and at other times of the Aegean and it's outlying islands. Nobody had seen any sign of activity or life down below, although there were ocassional glimpses of boats and yachts apparently bobbing about directionless and unmanned. Two hours had almost passed when Carl's voice came through the headphones to the other five. "Okay guys, it's almost two hours. We can either head back to Athens or, we're only a short distance from Heraklion Airport on Crete. We could put down there, have a look around and head back to Athens tomorrow. What do we all think?". There was a short babbling of voices as everyone discussed the pros and cons. Eventually they decided to put down on Crete because it was closer and the day was slipping away from them. It was now almost 4pm so they decided to land, find a plush hotel, cook up a good meal and get a good nights sleep and pray that the power station on Crete was still operating. This decided, Carl started to descend and circle the island to look for the airport to ensure that it wasn't blocked by a crashed or damaged plane. Easy to spot on the Northwest coast of the island, the airport runway was free of all traffic.

Carl brought the small plane into a final descent and smoothly touched down and taxied over to the airport terminal building. They all disembarked leaving the keys in the plane and the doors unlocked. "Who's going to steal it?" pointed out Carl, shrugging his shoulders at the others. They made their way around the side of the building and out onto the front area where there was the inevitable jam of stalled and crashed cars. At the front of the jumble of mainly taxis and minibuses, was a minibus with all doors open, a pile of suitcases at the rear loading door and a scattering of clothes all around it. Mike sauntered up and announced that the keys were in it. "Must have just been loading their luggage as it happened" he said as he turned the key in the ignition, not starting it but checking that it had fuel. "Come on everyone, it's got fuel. Let's go and find a hotel" he said.

CHAPTER EIGHT

Everyone climbed into the minibus and Mike took the driver's seat. As they skirted the stalled traffic and made their way out of the airport, Hannah, who had plumped for the front passenger seat shouted out to everyone "look, over there in that field" she pointed out of the passenger window with her left arm at something in a field off to the left of the road. "It looks like a dead sheep or goat to me" she said, "slow down Mike". Mike dutifully slowed the vehicle to a walking pace and they all peered out across the field at the fluffy bundle of something about 20 metres away from them. Sure enough it was a goat, its fluffy woolen hair agitating slightly in the gentle breeze but otherwise, laid flat and not moving. Mike stopped the vehicle and with an order to everyone to stay where they were he hopped over the flimsy barbed wire fence and trudged through the ankle high, tinder dry yellowing grass to wear the goat lay. He leaned over the animal and prodded it but he could see from it's glazed opaque eyes and dry leathery tongue which lolled from the side of its mouth that it was some time since this particular goat had drawn its last breath.

He returned to the minibus and announced to the others "it's dead. Looks like it has been for a couple of days. I wonder why it hasn't disappeared like everything else though". Carl offered, "perhaps whatever it was, Gamma Rays or whatever only affects living tissue?" Mike returned "could be, but all of the plants seem to be okay. It only seems to have affected animals, insects, birds and things like that. We saw loads of fish that were still okay when it happened. Did you?"

"We did" replied Mandy "so obviously any land animals that just happened to be underwater at the same depth as us should be okay as well – seals, birds diving for fish, certain reptiles....what do you think?" Everyone agreed that it would probably be the case and Mike started the minibus off again in search of somewhere for them to rest for the evening.

Their original plan had been for a hotel but they passed a long avenue lined with beautiful Bougainvillea trees on either side behind which lay the most eacuisite white villas with red terracotta roof tiles. They chose the one that looked the most extravagant and drove up the winding, red tarmac driveway past a fantastic tennis court and swimming pool complex which everyone cheered. They piled out of the minibus and dared each other into the pool. The boys stripped down to their boxers and the girls to their underwear. Lucy and Hannah weren't wearing bras which got a hoot from the guys and soon they were all cooling down in the cool azure blue water, frolicking and splashing each other, their predicament, for the time being at least, forgotten.

When they had had their fill of the pool they all went over to the front door of the villa which was unlocked. They split up into different factions and went exploring. It was a huge place with cool marble floors and expensive cut glass chandeliers, decorated throughout in brilliant white with luxuriant leather sofas and deep mahogany furniture. There turned out to be six bedrooms. Each couple picked a room and there was half an hour of pandemonium as they searched through the drawers and wardrobes in each others rooms for dry clothes that would fit them. Eventually they all got kitted out in an assortment of shorts, t-shirts and summer dresses and everyone convened in the bright chrome and teak kitchen which Tom announced was fitted out better than most restaurant kitchens.

In the freezer they found lots of steaks, sausages and burgers which, although the power had been off, were still very cold, some even a bit frozen in the middle. As they laid them out on the kitchen bench, Carl went in search of a barbecue and some charcoal. The girls hunted for candles for later on when it got dark and Lucy started to make a big bowl of salad from the contents of the huge, doubled doored stainless steel fridge. "Beers are still cold in here everyone" she shouted out and soon everyone was sipping a cold beer as they worked towards getting dinner ready. As they unwrapped the steaks Lucy pointed out "Mike was right what he said about this thing only affecting living tissue.......otherwise......well, these steaks – they wouldn't be here either would they?"

Everyone agreed with her – Carl had found a barbecue which was gas fired and had started it up and soon they were grilling meat outside on the patio area that led off from the kitchen and overlooked the pool and the tennis court. Mike, the ever resourceful pub landlord had managed to locate the previous owner's wine supply. The night was pleasantly passed with good food, plenty to drink and lots of drunken speculation about what had happened to the planet and what they were going to do about it.

They were all sat around in sun loungers and patio chairs, empty plates scattered over the patio table and floor and empty beer bottles and wine bottles dotted around when Mandy looked up at the sky and said "Isn't it a beautiful night? Look how clear the sky is and how many stars there are". Everyone looked up, almost as a single entity and nodded or agreed with Mandy apart from Carl. "Well it's not quite *that* perfect is it?" he said. "What do you mean?" asked Mandy.

"Well, about 3 or 4 nights ago we sat on the deck of the yacht in a little bay with a G & T, remember? And we were looking at the sky and the stars and we commented on........."

"Oh my god, that's right", interjected Mandy "it was a fantastic full moon".

"That's right" agreed Carl "and where is it now? It's a clear sky and it should be visible and only slightly eclipsed – just a bit more than three quarters full". Tom chirped in, "you don't suppose that it's been hit by something and that the collision and explosion was the flash that we all experienced, do you?"

"Oh come on guys, get real" mocked Mike. "If that was the case surely we would have had huge chunks of rock raining down on the planet from the collision". Carl countered, "not necessarily Mike. If the moon was on the other side of Earth at the time, which it was because we were in daylight, then if there was any debris it would have landed on the other side. That's if there was any debris. If the collision was so huge, perhaps the moon was just vaporized into dust".

"No, no, no" said Mike in disbelief "it can't be". Carl drove home his point and said "Well, where's the moon then mate? 'Cos I can't see it and it should be up there. And another thing; if the moon is destroyed we're going to be in a world of shit in the next few weeks".

Now the girls joined in, virtually in unison. "Why Carl. What will happen if the moon is missing?" all three of them asked together, quite spookily.

"Well I'm not a scientist or astrologist but I remember from the sciences at school that the moon controls a few things on Earth such as tides, gravity and the speed at which the Earth spins on its axis. So, there'll be no tides.....I don't know how that will affect us. The cycle of day and night will become shorter, about 9 or 10 hours. The Earth will gradually start to spin faster because it has no longer got the gravitational pull of the Moon to slow it down. This will mean that weather patterns will change.....I think it will become very windy but I'm not too sure on that one.....and also, because we're spinning faster the

Earth's gravitational pull will be weakened so we'll end up with something like the gravity of the Moon. In other words the Earth is spinning fast and trying to chuck us off the surface by centrifugal force and the only thing holding us down is gravity. We'd better pray that the two forces find equilibrium".

There was a long drawn out silence as they all pondered what Carl had said. Then Mike chirped up, trying to lighten the moment, "yeah, but that's all conjecture, isn't it. I mean we don't even know if the moon is actually missing yet do we?"

No-one answered him and they all eventually made their excuses and said goodnight to each other and finally lurched off to bed in the early hours. Mike said to everyone, in all seriousness "Well, I don't care. I know it's probably as near as we're going to come to it being the end of the world.... but I quite like it I don't mind telling you". They all tottered off to their own bedrooms, each harboring their own views on Mike's thoughts.

CHAPTER NINE

The next morning, Carl was the first to awake. He'd slept very little during the night, his mind actively going over and over the possibilities and the consequences if in fact the Moon had been hit by an asteroid or some other body from space. As Mandy slept peacefully next to him, her long blond hair falling over her tanned face, snoring slightly because she'd had a few glasses of wine, he wondered what precautions they should begin to take as a group just in case the scenario he had painted the night before was correct. Which part of the world would be best protected against the weather patterns that might emerge? Would there be widespread flooding because there were no tides? Would they have to weigh themselves down so they didn't go flying off into the atmosphere as the Earth spun faster? What would they eat after the reserves of canned and dried food had run out?

Eventually he realized he wasn't going to get any sleep so he got up, pulled on a pair of shorts and went downstairs to the kitchen. He really needed a strong cup of coffee to sharpen his senses and to help him think. The de-caff could go on the back burner for a while he decided. He hunted around in the kitchen cupboards until he found a jar of instant coffee then flipped the switch on the kettle, immediately realized that there was no power, so instead, filled a saucepan with water from the tap and turned on the gas hob. As the water came to the boil he heaped a teaspoon of coffee into a mug and wondered to himself how long the water would keep flowing from the taps and how much longer it would be safe to drink. Obviously there were no people around to man the filtration plants that ensured the purity of the water so how long would it be okay. "Well, I've boile it now" he thought to himself, and poured the water into the mug and carried it outside onto the patio.

The previous evening's debris had been cleared away and Lucy was sat down at the table drinking a bottle of spring water and reading her book. "I just couldn't sleep" she said "so I tidied up and stacked everything in the kitchen. I don't know why really. There wasn't much point under the circumstances, but......." she trailed off. "I know" replied Carl "it's going to be strange for a while adjusting to things. As soon as the others get up we need to have a good chat about what we're going to do. I've got some ideas that I'd like to run past everyone. Why don't you make yourself a coffee? I've just boiled some water on the stove". Lucy went into the kitchen, made herself a coffee and came back and sat at the patio table opposite Carl. They began to chat and Carl told her basically the 'Carl and Mandy' life story to date. "What about you and Tom?" he asked "how did you meet?"

Lucy recounted a brief life history explaining that she had met Tom when she was in training as a nurse at St. Thomas' Hospital on the south side of Westminster Bridge and Tom had been a probationary Police Constable at Cannon Row Police Station just the other side of the bridge at the top of Whitehall. This was about 5 years ago. They had met at 'pound a pint' night at the legendary 'Papagayo' night club just off Oxford Street and had hit it off straight away. After a few months Tom had moved out of the Police section house in Soho where he lodged with about 300 other single Police Officers and Lucy had quit her room in the 3 bedroom flat she shared with two other nurses in Hammersmith. Together they now rented a one bedroom flat in Ealing, not far from Mike and Hannah's pub, where they spent a lot of their free evenings, either in the bar or in the upstairs flat that Mike and Hannah lived in. The four had met while on a British Sub Aqua Club, class two diving course 4 years ago on the island of Malta and been best friends ever since. It was on that course that they all discovered that they only live a few hundred yards away from each other. Tom was now a firearms expert in the Met and Lucy was a fully qualified SRN. They planned to get married when they had saved up enough for a deposit on a house or flat in London but that was proving to be a lot more difficult than it sounded due to the explosive rate at which property prices were rising in the capital.

"Anyway" finished Lucy "that's enough about us. I'm going in for a morning dip. Are you coming?"

Carl replied "No thanks, I'm going to wait for the others to get up and have a scout around in the kitchen and see what there is for breakfast. You go ahead". Lucy headed off to the pool and Carl entered the patio doors into the kitchen and started looking through the cupboards and the fridge. He found lots of fresh fruit in the bottom of the fridge which still seemed okay and bread and eggs in one of the cupboards. He started to whisk up a load of eggs to make scrambled eggs and put a larger saucepan on the stove to make fresh coffee. As he worked the other four tripped down the stairs in dribs and drabs, in various states of dress, with tousled hair and bleary eyes. "I feel a bit rough" said Mike. "How many bottles of wine did we get through last night?" he asked. "Quite a few" said Carl, "sit down and there'll be some coffee ready in a minute and some scrambled eggs. Best I could manage at short notice I'm afraid?"

After ten minutes they were all seated at the large kitchen table and everyone had a mug of coffee, scrambled eggs and crusty bread and butter. Carl opened the conversation with "Okay, I have a plan and I want to know what everyone thinks of it but I also want to hear what ideas everyone else has....so get your thinking caps on. If we want to meet up with other people and reform a community we will have to go somewhere where all of the people, or at least most of them would have been protected from the 'flash'. I can't think of anywhere in the world where a huge number of people would have been underwater all at one time but I do know of somewhere where a huge number of people would have been underground".

"Where's that then Carl?" asked Tom "because I've been racking my brains and I could only think of tourists in caves and miners....and both of those groups would probably have dissipated and gone their separate ways once they resurfaced".

"I thought of that too and reached the same conclusion", replied Carl, "but I once read about this place in Australia called.........something like Coober Pedy....... and it is a whole town in the Opal mining area that is built underground and there are about 3500 inhabitants. I think that as well as all the shops, businesses, bars and restaurants being underground about 70% of the population of approximately 3500 people also live underground. So that would be my suggestion. I'm confidant that Mandy and I could get us there......so ......any comments?"

There was silence for a few moments then Mike spoke up. "I'm not saying yeah or nay at this stage Carl but some factors that we're going to have to consider if everything we suspect about the moon and the tides and all that is true. We're going to have to live near a source of protein and at the minute I can only think of fish, so that means near the sea or a lake. We need to be on reasonably high ground in case of flooding because we don't know what kind of result there will be with no tides. It will need to be well sheltered because of the high winds that we assume will follow in due course and we also need to be near a large town or city so that we can resupply with food, bottled water, generators, fuel and all other types of essentials. Also, we need to be on arable ground so that we can grow crops, fruit and vegetables because the supermarkets will only keep us going for 2 or 3 years with canned and dried goods. How does Coober Pedy measure up to all of those factors because I've never heard of it and I've no idea where in Australia it is?"

"You've raised some good points there Mike" replied Carl. "I think Coober Pedy is well inland and doesn't really match up to any of your criteria. But there will be benefits – other people, a community, power, doctors, hospital..... lots of things that we're going to need in the future which we won't have if we 'go it alone'.

Mandy was listening intently to the discussion. A doctor was quite high on her list of priorities. This morning she had secretly taken the ClearBlu pregnancy test she had lifted from the supermarket in Athens. The 2 minute wait after she had peed on the stick seemed like an eternity and she turned over in her mind all the visits to doctors over the years that had assured her there was nothing physically preventing them having children. Could it be true? Could she at last suddenly be pregnant? The answer lay in the little window three quarters of the way down the white plastic strip she held in her hand. It had turned blue indicating that she was indeed pregnant after all these years. Although she was ecstatic she had managed to contain her excitement and wait for the right time to let Carl know the good news.

The conversation carried on around her. Mike, being backed up now by Tom and the two girls, although not in a confrontational way, was arguing that somewhere in the Mediterranean would be best. As he pointed out "The Med has no tides already so that aspect won't be a problem. The climate is perfect....at the moment. The Med is prolific with fish and wildlife and most places you go you can see grapes growing, oranges, lemons, olives, melons. We can find the ideal location near a big town somewhere and really set ourselves up properly in fantastic houses. Get generators and fuel sorted out and huge supplies of bottled water and dried and canned food......I think we'd be crazy to try flying half way around the world just to find other people. Just my opinion".

Having thought about what the other four had said, Carl was beginning to believe that their option would be best all round. It was a hell of a risk to fly half way around the globe in a small single engine plane. There were weather factors and navigational and fuel difficulties to overcome plus the fact that they would have to do it in 4-5 hour hops to be safe. It could take them 3 or 4 days. As he was deliberating, Mandy decided that now was as good a time as any to share her news with everyone because she was definitely going to need the help of a doctor. Carl knew his way around the uterus of many animals but she definitely did not want their first child to be delivered by a vet. "I have something I'd like to add" she interjected. Everyone looked at her and, although the situation was pretty grim she couldn't help but burst out into a wide grin as she informed everyone "I think I'm pregnant".

After a short, stunned silence, during which time Carl's jaw nearly hit the floor, everyone suddenly erupted into a cacophony of congratulations and Carl hugged Mandy to him ferociously almost knocking the wind from her, with a from grin ear to ear that was so wide his jaw was in danger of dropping off. He whispered into her ear so that only she could hear "Well done darling. I love you so much. I knew we could do it". She could barely hear him above the congratulations and back slapping of the other four but she gave him a tight squeeze back in acknowledgement before they broke apart and shook hands and accepted kisses from Tom, Mike, Lucy and Hannah.

"Well this definitely calls for an end to current discussions and a celebration" shouted Mike, and like the good pub landlord he was he disappeared for a few seconds and came back sporting two bottles of Bollinger. "Champers" he announced "not chilled I'm afraid but under the circumstances who gives a monkeys?"

"Mike" said Hannah "it's only ten thirty in the morning!". "I know" he replied "but it's a very special occasion and anyway, there is no wrong time of the day to drink champagne". He found some champagne flutes in one of the glass fronted kitchen cabinets and poured a glass for everyone except Mandy who he limited to half a glass. There were cheers all round and the clinking of glasses. "Er, guys.... I don't want to be the voice of doom or anything" chirped up Mandy, "but I don't want to go through this pregnancy and birth without a doctor or at least a midwife being there at the birth. I want us to seek out some other people in the hope of finding some professional medical help and I think Coober Pedy seems like a good idea. Perhaps we could persuade a few people to come back to the Med with us.....you know..... a few people of different professions to start up a new community here". This started up the good natured debate again and the group talked on for the best part of the morning, although Lucy did point out to Mandy that she was a nurse and felt confident she could deliver the baby and any pre-natal and post-natal care required.

The outcome was that Mike, Hannah, Tom and Lucy would stay here on Crete while Carl and Mandy flew to Coober Pedy with the intention of returning within a couple of weeks with or without any other people who wanted to come with them. Carl was sure that Coober Pedy had an airstrip and lots of private pilots. If they couldn't get a doctor or nurse to come back with them, then they would arm themselves with as much knowledge as possible from those professions in Coober Pedy to be confident of a safe delivery back on Crete when the baby was eventually born. They all agreed that they would first of all explore the island, pick out the best three villas for themselves and get power to them with generators. They would stock them up with fuel, food and water and other essentials and then, in about a week's time they would see Carl and Mandy off at the airport. While all this was happening Carl would take a trip out to the airport to ensure that the plane was okay. He would try and find the plane's documentation in the airport offices and check that it had been recently serviced. He would also refuel it from one of the many fuel tankers dotted around the airfield and also pick up the relevant aviation maps from the airport offices as they were obviously going to get no help from any satellite navigation instruments on board the plane. They would plan their route and their fuel stops carefully and only set off when they were 100% sure that they had covered every angle and eventuality.

This decided, they agreed that rather than go scouring the island for accommodation they would check out the other villas in the neighborhood, as it did appear to have been a very affluent area. They all dived into the minibus and with Tom at the wheel this time they went exploring. The villa they had been occupying was called Villa Mercedes, Lucy informed them, as she pointed out the terracotta and white printed sign adorning the whitewashed wall just to the left of the ornate double gates, which were mate of black wrought iron and "would have cost a bleeding fortune" according to Tom. "Can we look out for one with a Porsche in the drive?" asked Mike, "I've always wanted a Porsche". As they progressed up the tree lined avenue with the villas on their right and the sea on their left, it became apparent that they had sold themselves short the previous evening. They were passing villas now that dwarfed Villa Mercedes, making it look like a small 'two up, two down' in comparison. Tom pointed out that Mike could take his pick. They were now obviously in what had once been a very wealthy area and nearly every drive was littered with Porsches, Mercedes, BMWs and Audis. Mike was like a terrier with a bone, chafing at the bit to be out of the car and in amongst the prestige cars on every driveway.

They came to an area where the road swept away from the sea in a long slow curve and started to go uphill slightly. As they rounded the corner they could see ahead of them a few hundred yards up the hill a group of half a dozen villas that stood out from all the others. They were all brilliant white, almost too bright in the mid morning sun and had red terracotta tiled roofs. Although each was slightly different in shape, they all looked as if the had been designed by the same architect because they were built in a style slightly reminiscent of small palaces. "What about these?" Tom asked, already anticipating what the response would be. "These look great" said Mandy, "bagsy the one with the nicest nursery".

Tom stopped the minibus at the foot of the driveway of the first villa and everyone tumbled out in excitement. "Let's split up and look around and choose one each" he said, "then we'll meet back here at the minibus in.....say....one hour?" Everyone agreed and they split into couples and went off as excited as schoolchildren on a field trip knowing that they had no lessons that day.

Mike and Hannah headed straight up the driveway of the villa outside which they had stopped; Mike grabbing Hannah's hand and pulling her along almost sweeping her off her feet. "What's the hurry?" she asked, "it's not going anywhere". "I know, I know" he responded, "but look.....just behind that huge tree....a Porsche Boxster and a Porsche Cayenne. It's a double whammy". They walked up the long driveway which was lined with a variety of pine tree that Hannah did not know the name of but appreciated the scent and the cool shade they offered from the late morning Mediterranean sun. As they approached the front of the house the cars were parked on the gravel driveway and they could see the cool blue water of a swimming pool just around the back of the house to the right hand side. Mike started looking at the cars while Hannah went inside the house by the front door which had been left not only unlocked but also slightly ajar. She walked around leisurely, surprised by how cool it was compared to the heat outside, admiring the ornate marble tiles on the floors and walls almost throughout the whole house. As she wandered through, she fell in love with the place. It had 6 bedrooms, all en-suite with walk in wardrobes. The double patio doors of the huge living room opened up onto a lush green lawn and the huge swimming pool. As she strolled, she thought to herself how hard it would be to keep the grass green and the swimming pool correctly chlorinated. In fact there were a lot of things they were all going to have to learn to do for themselves now that they were living in a world where one could no longer just pick up the phone and call on the services of a professional in any particular field.

The kitchen was magnificent with cool grey flecked marble tiling throughout and light oak paneling and doors. In the centre was an island with preparation area, hobs and sinks and in the corner of the room a door opened off into another area that was pitch black. Hannah walked over to this area and looked through the door into the gloom. It was obviously a cellar because she could see stairs leading downwards and could feel cool air with a slightly musty but not altogether unpleasant smell, a bit like.....what was it? Wine....? Reluctant to go down into the dark alone, she shouted out for Mike. "No need to shout" he answered, startling her because he was in the kitchen just behind her. "I found the keys for the cars in that drawer over there. What have you found?" She replied, "it might be a wine cellar. Have a look for some matches or candles and we'll go and have a look." At the mention of 'wine cellar' Mike momentarily forgot about his two new toys on the driveway, pocketed the keys and started scrabbling through the kitchen drawers. He came back with a candle which he had lit from one of the hobs, informing Mandy that they were gas and not electric which would be a bonus until they could get the power up and running. Together they descended the steps to the cellar and as they reached the bottom the flickering light from the candle picked up the racks and racks of wine lining the two longest walls which ran off to the right. Down the centre of the cellar, between the thousands of bottles of wine, all stored in neat little terracotta circles, was a long solid wood table flanked by two benches either side. The room was cool and looked like it had seen many a night of revelry. "This swings it for me" commented Mike. "The house is great, it's got a pool, two Porsches and now a wine cellar fit for a king. Do you like it babe?" he asked. "I love it" she replied, turning and hugging him. "If we're going to start a new life then this is the perfect place for me". They walked back out of the cellar and out through the living room doors to the pool. "We'll have to get the pump and filters working as soon as possible" noted Mike "or the water will start to go green with algae. Come on, let's try out the Boxster and go and meet up with the others. It's been almost an hour". They climbed into the small compact sports car; Mike started the engine first time, lowered the hood with the electric switch and drove down the driveway of their new home to meet up with their friends.

CHAPTER TEN

Back at the minibus Carl and Hannah looked suitably impressed with Mike's new Porsche. They had driven down from their new 'humble abode' in a large 4 wheel drive BMW X4 which Mike had a good look at before assuring himself that his Porsche was much better. "No sign of Tom and Lucy yet?" asked Hannah. "Not yet", replied Mandy, "but the hour is up so they should be here any minute". As she spoke a silver grey Mercedes saloon came flying out of a driveway further up the hill, turned onto the road with a screech of tyres and sped towards them. It came to a very abrupt halt just beside the four of them and they could see that only Tom was in the vehicle. "Quick you lot, follow me. You'll never believe what we have found in our house", he blurted and immediately turned the car in the road and sped off back up the road and turned left into the driveway again. The others, more than intrigued, climbed into their respective vehicles and chased after him.

As they all pulled up at the front of the villa that Tom and Lucy had been checking out, they just spotted Tom dashing in through the front door. They followed in behind him and all four stopped dead in their tracks and stared in disbelief at the sight of Lucy sat on the bottom two steps of the elegant marble and brass stairway with a litlle girl of about six or seven years old sat on her knee chattering away to her in English with a hint of a Spanish accent. "Hi you guys", said Lucy, "I'd like to introduce you to Manuela. She was playing in the cellar a couple of days ago and when she came up for a drink to the kitchen her mum, dad and brother were missing."

"I can't find them anywhere", the little girl chirped up. "I've been crying a lot because I've been to all the other houses and I can't find anyone and the phones and lights don't work….and….I'm starving". Tom said, "she's quite a little chatterbox, aren't you Manuela?".

"My mum always used to say that too. Can we have something to eat now please?" she replied. Lucy wandered off to the kitchen with her and Tom pulled the others together and began to tell them the story of what had happened. He and Lucy had been exploring the house when they heard some mumbling from one of the bedrooms. They cautiously went in and found Manuela sitting on her bed talking to a group of her dolls. The house had a two level cellar and the bottom level had been turned into a playroom for Manuela and her brother to play in when they were back in Spain from bording school in England for the school holidays. She had been playing down there when the flash had occurred obviously. The rest of the family had disappeared but one of them had…. well…. not quite disappeared.

To explain better what he meant, Tom took them all through the kitchen, where Lucy was taking food from cupboards in an attempt to find out what Manuela would and would not eat. He led them down the stairs to the cellar and at the bottom of the first flight of stairs on the upper level of the cellar was a pile of clothes – a short blue skirt, flip flops, white thong knickers and a blue sleeveless top. However, the clothes weren't just a pile on the floor. There was something in them that, at first, the group could not identify. Tom illuminated them. There was a mass of flesh and skin about the size of a large pumpkin with short stubby protrusions. The skin was very red and burnt looking and the protrusions were a bit like the flippers on a seal or sea lion. A mop of long dark hair, thinned out and straggly flopped over one side of the thing that, upon closer inspection, resembled a badly deformed human torso. "I think we're looking at the remains of Manuela's mum here" announced Tom. "Those flipper things must have been her arms and legs at one time. I reckon she must have been in a kind of 'dead zone' when the flash occurred. Another metre up the steps and she would have been totally nuked or whatever and if she had made it down the steps another metre or two she may well have been okay, like Manuela. That's what I think anyway".

After a few seconds of stunned silence Carl ventured "It must have been an awful way to die for billions of people….we should all thank our lucky stars that we're still here by a fluke of circumstance really. Do you think we should bury it…her, I mean?". They all agreed that they should and Tom disappeared back up the cellar stairs to the kitchen and came back with a binliner. "I know it's not very dignified", he said, "but let's just get rid of it. It's giving me the creeps. There must be thousands of bodies just like this all around the world. People who weren't quite far enough into a tunnel or into a cave or a cellar. People swimming, snorkelling or diving who weren't quite deep enough…..doesn't bear thinking about". The three men took the bin bag of human remains out to the rear of the garden and dug a shallow grave in the soft earth below a thick pine tree with a spade Tom had found in a tool shed in the garden. They placed the bag gently in and scraped the soil back over the top. No-one said a word as they came back into the kitchen to find the three girls engaging Manuela in conversation, re-assuring her that she was fine now because she was with new friends who would take care of her.

While Manuela quietly chewed her way through a peanut butter sandwich complemented with a bag of crisps and a drink of orange cordial the six new friends had a quick tete a tete about what they should do with her. Tom and Lucy said that they didn't mind looking after her and staying in this house as it was them that had found her and she had taken quite a shine to Lucy. Everyone agreed but also agreed that she was now the overall responsibility of all of them. Lucy pointed out that she would come in useful to them if they met any locals who had survived the flash because she was fluent in both English and Greek. Manuel had told Lucy and Tom that her mum was 'a bit Spanish and a bit English' (hence the name Manuela probably) and her dad was Greek. She went to St. Elphin's Boarding School for Girls in Darley Dale, Derbyshire and came back to Crete on school holidays. She was seven years old and had been very scared over the last couple of days, surviving on pop and crisps.

Carl, Tom and Mike decided that a priority for them was to try and get power back on in the three villas they had chosen. To this end they decided they were going to scour the island for a builder's merchants or similar industrial type property that stocked a range of generators that would be powerful enough to supply a large house. They were obviously going to need three of them so they set off in the newly acquired BMW X4 as it was now lunch time and they didn't know how long it was going to take them. The three girls, well, three and a half girls now, decided to find a large supermarket and stock up on as much food, drink, candles, torches and other necessities as they could lay their hands on. Both groups decided to meet back up at Tom, Lucy and Manuela's villa before it got dark.

The three guys drove back towards the airport because Carl had commented that he'd seen a large industrial area close to it. They struck lucky more or less straight away as they entered the first avenue on the Industrial Park and found a huge yard full of tarmac lorries, steamrollers and generators of all types and sizes, most of which were built onto trailers. They parked up and walked up and down the rows of trailers scanning the generator specifications on each one, until Mike finally said, "let's face it lads, we haven't got a clue what we're looking for have we?" Carl replied, "Well I'm assuming we want something that outputs 220 to 240 volts and looks substantial enough to power a house. I don't know what all this stuff is on the specifications about Amps and Wattage but I'm sure we'll learn by our mistakes if we don't get the right one first time. We're going to have to look for a vehicle in this yard that can tow one of these things because the BMW doesn't have a tow bar".

They split up – Carl to the yard office to look for the cupboard or drawer where the vehicle keys would be kept and the other two to search for a vehicle with a tow bar. Carl found a neat, metallic clipboard on the wall of the office, the door of which had been left open. He silently thanked the neat and tidy office manager who had laboriously labeled the rows and rows of keys with tags indicating the vehicle and its registration number, or in the case of the generators, by their serial numbers. Between the three of them they married up the keys to a large DAF truck that was usually used to transport molten tarmac and a huge dark green generator about the size of a large trailer tent. They also found a small tanker full of diesel with its own onboard generator for pumping fuel. Once the generator was coupled up to the DAF they threw as many different cables as they could find into the back and the strange convoy of BMW, tanker and DAF towing the generator set off slowly back in the direction of the new homes they had adopted.

When they arrived back it was late afternoon. The girls had returned from their shopping spree or "shoplifting spree really" as Hannah pointed out. They were busy unloading the

Mercedes of their bounty as the strange convoy turned onto the driveway, causing a few giggles. The guys set straight to work positioning the generator, making sure it was full of fuel and examining the different output settings that it was capable of. They found a 3-core cable that fitted the output socket of the machine but the only problem was that it had a similar socket at the other end of it. Carl proposed that they just cut this socket off and marry up the three cables to the input on the main circuit board where the mains cables entered the house. After some trimming with Stanley knife and pliers found in a small tool box in the garden outhouse and much sweating and cursing under the breath they finally got the cables connected up to the mains input board. They found an earth spike and thick copper cable on the generator trailer and worked out how to ground the machine. Once they had done this they all stood around the machine looking at the rather complex control panel and settings, which thankfully were in English and not Greek. They decided to turn off all lights and appliances in the house first, then start the generator with the output settings on what they thought were the lowest possible to start with. This done, they called the girls out of the house "just in case" pointed out Carl and turned the key. The machine turned over a few times and spluttered into life, emitting a plume of thick black smoke before settling down into a dull, throbbing idle.

Everyone was tense, waiting for an explosion from the house but nothing happened. After a couple seconds the three guys told the girls to wait outside while they went in to try a few things out. They entered via the kitchen door and Carl said half jokingly, half nervously "right – fingers in ears just in case – I'm going to try the light switch first". He flipped the light switch and to everyone's amazement, the light came on straight away although not very bright. "By god" said Tom, "I think we've done it. Just need to turn the output switch up to the next level and we should be there. He went outside and after a couple of seconds Carl and Mike shouted out to him, "that's it, perfect", as the light increased in brightness to what a normal domestic light should be. Tom came back into the kitchen and said, "Now for the real test, lets try some of the appliances that we know use a lot of juice". They switched on the kettle – nothing blew up. They switched on the electric oven – nothing blew. They got confident and went around the house turning on light switches and appliances as they went and everything worked fine. "I really didn't think it would be that easy" said Carl. "Tomorrow we'll go and get another two of the same generator and set them up at the other houses. We'll have to check them daily for fuel and, perhaps we should bring an extra one as a spare because every few weeks we'll have to stop them and change oil, filters and stuff".

They all agreed that it would wait until tomorrow and called the girls back into the house. They all decided to sleep in this villa tonight as it had power and they all set to and unloaded the rest of the food and provisions and started the preparations for an evening meal. "Pasta in a cheesy, tomato sauce with canned tuna, garlic and onions" announced Lucy, "in my new kitchen!" Manuela announced that she loved pasta and after a short disappearing act, the ever resourceful Tom came back with his arms loaded with half a dozen bottles of red wine. They all mucked in together and half an hour later were sat around the huge solid pine kitchen table, eating, drinking and discussing the plans for tomorrow. The guys decided that they would get the other two houses powered up and the girls agreed that they would go to the airport and check on the plane, the refueling situation, the service history of the plane and try and find any aeronautical maps that Carl and Mandy might need.

The next couple of days were busy as the power gradually went on in each house and the three women started to make each house their own. Manuela turned out to be a little busybody and she flitted between the three houses, chattering away and doing little chores that she was given to keep her out of mischief. Carl and Mandy had worked out their route to include stops for refueling and it was agreed that they would leave on what turned out to be the seventh day after the flash. They were only going to fly in daylight and were going to navigate with the maps and using land features. They promised the others that whatever happened they would be back at the latest 3 weeks from today barring a mishap of some kind. Obviously there would be no chance of communication between them so if they did not return on the agreed date there would be no way of knowing what had happened but Carl and Mandy re-iterated that it was definitely their intention to return. If they didn't make it back for that date it would be for a reason that was out of their control and they would endeavor to return as soon as possible after that date. They were going to bring back as many people as they could muster – preferably people with skills and trades that would help them all built a new life together on Crete.

On the morning of departure the whole entourage drove in 3 vehicles to the airport and after refueling the plane and loading it up with food and drink and other goodies there was a series of goodbyes, handshakes, kisses and lots of tears. The little plane taxied away and the group of five watched as it sped down the runway and soared gracefully into the clear blue early morning Mediterranean skies. "Well", said Tom lightheartedly to try and brighten the mood, "They're doing their bit to try and rebuild the human race so I suggest that from tomorrow, now that we've sorted out the houses, we have a couple of days of searching the island and seeing if we can find anyone else still alive". Everyone agreed with him and they all piled back into the vehicles and drove off, leaving the BMW where it stood with the keys in the ignition in anticipation of the return of their friends in three weeks time.

CHAPTER ELEVEN

At the same time as the small plane soared gracefully away and the other friends departed the airport, Captain Wayne Toohey of The Royal Australian Navy Submarine Service made the unprecedented decision to disobey his Standing Orders. As skipper of HMAS Collins Class Conventional Submarine RANKIN he had been under strict guidelines for his current training exercise in the South Pacific Ocean. One of the main priorities of the exercise was under no circumstances was he to surface the boat unless a life threatening emergency occurred. The submarine was on a military and naval exercise. The top brass wanted to assess her capabilities for prolonged submersion duties and so far it had gone well. They had been submerged for a full forty eight days now and communications had been excellent with Naval HQ at HMAS Stirling in Rockingham on the west coast of Australia. However, several days ago all communications had ceased with HQ and further scans on all frequencies had not been able to illicit a response from anyone either military or civilian. Wayne wasn't unduly worried and it wasn't a 'life threatening' situation but he did feel, after discussions with his more senior officers, that they would be justified in surfacing to attempt to establish the cause of the problem and to see if it could be remedied at sea so that the exercise could continue.

Wayne summoned his Number Two, Lieutenant Josh Cransley, a small dark haired young man of 29 years with English parents and an accent that was very refined 'Aussie' due to the three years he had spent at Cambridge University in the late nineties. The wiry young man looked up at his direct superior – Wayne was tall for a submariner at over six feet and was well built due to his unshakeable love of Aussie Rules football which he played at every available opportunity when ashore. The two were very close friends but in the presence of other crew members it was a strictly professional relationship and Josh enquired of Wayne, "Yes sir?"
Wayne gave the order most of the crew had been anticipating for a couple of days now. "I want you to take her up Number Two. It's been over a week and HQ must be wondering what's happened with comms. I know it goes against our initial orders but I have made an entry in my log and I accept total responsibility for the decision if it turns out to be ill advised".
"Aye Sir" responded Josh as he about turned and headed to the Communication Console – the hub of the vessel - to give the order.

Minutes later the RANKIN broke clear of the deep blue and white flecked surface of the Pacific Ocean with a roar and gushing of turbulent waters that was totally silent below decks but deafening on the surface. The communications engineers were dispatched to the top deck to check the aerials, rigging and cabling for any obvious problems and other teams within the vessel set about the standard checks and duties associated with an unscheduled mid-mission re-surfacing. The vessel and the crew were run with ramrod precision and Wayne Toohey was very proud of his position, his boat and his crew.
"Soon have this problem sorted out and be back on our way" he thought to himself as he made his way up top for a few much needed breaths of fresh, sea air. Five months breathing nothing but air conditioned recycled air made one aware of what most people in the world took for granted. As he breathed his first few gulps of the rich ozone air he actually felt quite light headed and he turned his face towards the sun to savor the feel of it on his skin. Who knows when he would see it again?

CHAPTER TWELVE

At the same time as the vessel broke the surface of the water Carl and Mandy were a couple of hours into the last leg of their journey. All landings, refueling, overnight stays and take offs had gone without incident, although they had encountered no other survivors so far on their three day trip. This was the final few hours of the journey which should see them safely into the small dirt airfield at Coober Pedy sometime later that afternoon. Both were apprehensive and there was a contemplative silence in the cockpit of the small plane as they both harbored their own thoughts about what they might find when they landed. Mandy was looking out of the passenger side cockpit window, lost in thought when she saw an eruption in the deep blue of the ocean below. There was a huge spume of white foam and spray followed by what looked like a very large missile erupting from the surface of the water. She sat bolt upright and said to Carl "Look at that, down there Carl. It looks like.....could it be....a submarine?" Carl looked down just as the submarine had reached it's full upward traverse and was settling down to a horizontal and stationary position. "My God" he exclaimed. "It is a submarine. I'll circle around and go a bit lower. You start trying all the frequencies on the radio – every channel. If there's anyone there they should be able to hear us."

Mandy turned the radio receiver knob to position one of sixty four, depressed the pressle switch that activated her headset microphone and spoke into the mic. "Unidentified submarine – this is Mandy Rutherford of Cessna Stationair – SX ARG. Do you read me? Over" There was no immediate response so she repeated the salutation. There was still no response so she changed the knob to channel two and repeated the procedure. As Carl kept the plane in a tight circle above the slow moving submarine, Mandy kept up the methodical repeating and channel switching and as she got to channel 27 they both noticed that the hatches on the fore and aft towers of the submarine were simultaneously opening and people were spilling out onto the turreted raised decks. The sailors on deck spotted the plane and began waving. Mandy persevered with her radio procedures and on channel thirty two she had a breakthrough and a rich Australian voice answered. "G'day Mandy. This is HMAS Rankin. Go ahead – over."

Mandy and Carl beamed at each other as Mandy proceeded to introduce themselves. The operator onboard the sub explained to her that they had surfaced to check out their communications systems because they had lost comms with the outside world about 12 days ago and assumed there must be a problem with the kit on deck. Mandy told the operator to put the Commanding Officer on the radio and as Wayne Toohey took the mic and introduced himself, Mandy recounted the events of the last twelve days to him, including their theory of a strike of some sort on the Moon and the subsequent consequences. This took some time to sink in with Wayne who said to Mandy over the air "just give me a few minutes Mandy. I'll be right back. Over".

Wayne called for his number two and they sat down together in Josh's bunk while Wayne broke the news to him that Mandy had relayed to him. Between them they decided that their best plan of action was to proceed to Rockingham as one of the other submarines in the fleet was also on maneuvers at the same time as them and that submarine, HMAS Collins would no doubt also be heading back to Rockingham. Wayne then jumped back on the radio to Mandy and informed her what they were going to do. She informed him of their plan to go to Coober Pedy. Wayne was sceptical but said nothing. He personally thought that nearly every inhabitant of Coober Pedy would by now have headed for the coast as Coober Pedy was reliant on transporters bringing almost everything into the town required for human survival. After twelve days or so, stocks of almost everything would have been running low. Realising that Carl and Mandy were too far committed to their journey to change their plans now anyway, he said nothing but did invite them to carry on after Coober Pedy to Rockingham where they would be made very welcome. He gave Mandy his address at the Naval Base then both groups said their goodbyes and wished each other luck and Carl turned the plane back towards the Australian mainland

and began his ascent back to cruising altitude. Wayne came up on deck and watched the small plane climb away and fade into the distance. "They'll find out about Coober Pedy soon enough" he thought to himself, as he pondered how he was going to break the catastrophic news to the crew of forty five men, and contemplated what their reaction would be. At least he now knew that his radio comms were working, even if all satellite systems were off line, so he could have his radio operators on constant monitoring and tracking of the frequencies.....just in case.

CHAPTER THIRTEEN

Back in the cockpit of the little plane Carl and Mandy discussed the possibility of travelling on to Rockingham after Coober Pedy. Mandy started the ball rolling by saying "it would be very reassuring if we went there and there were the crews of two submarines that had survived. It would fill me with a lot more confidence about the future".
"I agree" said Carl "but it would worry me taking you there as the only female with about a hundred or so blokes around, all of them having been at sea for several weeks.........you see where I'm going with this?" She replied "yeah, I know......tell you what ....let's reserve judgment until we see what it's like in Coober Pedy, okay?"
"Okay" agreed Carl "Should be there in about 4 hours now".

They spent the rest of the journey discussing 'what ifs' and speculating on what they would find when they got there. One thing they agreed on was that, if they were going to take anybody back to Heraklion with them, they would have to find themselves a bigger plane or they would be limited to just a couple of people. This could be done either at Coober Pedy airfield if there were any planes left there, or by flying on to somewhere else and picking one up if the numbers warranted it.

They crossed the Australian coast about an hour later and two and a half hours later Carl started his descent and approach to Coober Pedy's dusty dirt strip of a runway. From this altitude there was no sign of life and not one other plane anywhere to be seen on the airfield. "Nothing to worry about" assured Carl when Mandy pointed this out to him. "Don't forget, they live underground".

They landed as smoothly as was possible on the bumpy landing strip and taxied over to the small building that seemed to serve as a terminal. Carl decided that it would be best if they refueled the plane before they did anything else, just in case anything untoward should happen and they needed to get away quick. As on all their previous stops this was not a problem Full fuel tankers were parked up and the keys were readily available in the small office in the terminal building. They drove one of the tankers over to the Cessna and Mandy began the refueling as Carl unloaded a rucksack with a few bits and pieces in it that they though might be useful – sleeping bags, bottled water, a few sachets of food and a few toiletries. As Mandy was about halfway through the refueling process they were both startled by a shout from about fifty yards away where a huge bearded man had seemingly appeared from nowhere. "What the bloody hell do you think you're doing there mate?" he boomed. Dressed in khaki shorts, desert boots, a khaki shirt and a felt hat with the widest brim they'd ever seen, he strode purposefully towards them, the face beneath the unkempt beard bright red either from too much sun or too much alcohol and his huge gut wobbling. Mandy had to suppress a girlish giggle as she took the sight in and thought to herself "it's Crocodile Dundee's uncle".

Carl turned and started to walk towards him and stuck out his right arm to offer a handshake as they approached each other. "Hello" Carl said. "I'm Carl Rutherford and that's Mandy, my wife" he said indicating Mandy with his left hand. "We were just refueling because we thought there was no-one around". The big Australian took Carl's hand in his and said "Mick Dwight – Mayor of Coober Pedy.....it's customary here in Australia to ask first mate, before you help yourself to something that isn't yours to take".

"We're really sorry" butted in Mandy "but we thought..... you know....under the circumstances that it would be okay. We didn't see anyone around".

"Oh don't worry about it – I'm only Joshing you mate" replied Mick. Carl and Mandy could see that he was a big man both in size and in persona and Mandy guessed he must be about 60 years old but still strong as an ox. "Come on, let's finish your refueling and get you down below out of this heat".

They finished off the refueling and Carl locked up the plane, pocketing the keys thinking to himself that he wanted to take no chances until he found out what the score was here. Mick led them down a dirt track where he'd parked up a 4 wheel drive Toyota Land cruiser just behind the spindly legs of what must have been the world's most rickety air traffic control building. They all climbed in and Mick drove for a few minutes until they reached one of the passageways that led to the first of the underground levels. During the brief journey Carl and Mandy told him their story and as they parked up in the cool of the underground car parking facility just above the first level of retail and domestic units. Mick said "come on, we'll go and have a cold drink, I'll introduce you to a few people and we'll tell you our story". This said, they descended another level down a brightly lit stairwell and came out through a set of double glass doors to what looked like any shopping mall in any city anywhere in the world. Mandy commented on the fact that there was electricity and Mick explained that the town's electricity was supplied by a generator farm which was still running okay because there was plenty of fuel left. He led them past a row of shops, most of which were completely devoid of any window dressings or stock of any kind, and into a small dimly lit bar called The Coober Cooler, where there was a group of six or seven people sat at the bar drinking cold beers and chatting.

CHAPTER FOURTEEN

At about the same time as Carl and Mandy drew up their bar stools in the Coober Cooler, Tom, Lucy, Mike, Hannah and Manuela were just returning from the beach a short drive down the hill from their new residences back on Crete. Walking back to the car they carried an assortment of beach towels, cooler boxes, masks, snorkels, flippers and fishing gear. They had had a very successful day. Lucy and Hannah had kept Manuela occupied with sandcastles, swimming, snorkeling and shell collecting while Tom and Mike had been doing the 'hunter gatherer' bit and excelled themselves with a fine catch of twelve large, fat grey mullet and two octopus. The fish had been caught on rod and line using stale bread as bait and Mike had caught the octopus by shoving his hand into their rocky underwater lairs, allowing them to grip his hand with their tentacles and then forcibly pulling them out. Once extracted, they had to be quickly turned inside out to kill them before the short powerful beak could do too much damage to Mike's hands.

The guys were suitably impressed with themselves. The group had lived on processed foods for many days now and were all craving fresh produce. Now that the protein side of the deal was accomplished they were all off to scour the fields for fresh fruit and vegetables. Throwing the gear into the back of the 4 x 4 they all climbed in and set off away from the beach heading clockwise around the island keeping the sea to their left.

"Everyone be on the lookout for anything growing that looks remotely edible" shouted Lucy above the noise of the wind blowing in through the open windows. They were passing through an area that was quite green, with small white huts dotted about in fields. The further they drove, veering inland slightly, the greener the landscape became, until little Manuela piped up, "here – this field here – it's got grapes in it – look". Tom pulled the car to a halt at the side of the road and everyone got out. Sure enough, it looked as if they'd just started at the border of a vineyard and fields of rich green vines stretched inland as far as the eye could see. "I'll just go and see if there's anything on the vines" volunteered Mike as he stepped across the drainage ditch into the first field. He grabbed a bunch of green grapes from the first vine he came to and brought them back to the group. Everyone tried a grape and everyone's face twisted into a grimace at the same time. "Not quite ripe" ventured Lucy through pursed lips and squinted eyes. "Perhaps another few weeks but at least we know where they are now for future reference".

"Oh well – onward and upward" shouted Tom. "Back in the car and let's carry on looking. We'll head inland a bit. We're bound to find some other fresh stuff". They all re-embarked the vehicle and set off once more following a small, winding single track road away from the shoreline and towards a distant set of hills that also looked lush and green a few miles distant. A mile or so on as they approached the lower slopes of the first set of hills, Hannah shouted "stop the car a moment and look up there". She pointed to the side of a hill with several small openings that looked like the mouths of small caves. It was several hundred metres away but Hannah was sure she had seen some small white objects moving around. "Can anyone else see those little white dots? Are they moving?" she enquired of the rest of the group. Everyone could see the little cluster of white dots but they did not appear to be moving to anyone else. "Can we get out and go and have a closer look?" she asked "because I'm sure I saw movement among them". Everyone agreed that they could so they all climbed out of the vehicle and headed across the fields, slightly uphill towards the cave entrances and the small group of little white objects.

As they approached the small white dots became larger and larger until it could be seen that they were actually moving slightly. "They're sheep aren't they?" asked Hannah. A few more steps and Tom said "No, they're goats – look at the horns on that big one"

Sure enough, with only a couple of hundred metres to go it was clear that it was a small flock of about twenty five or so, wooly white goats, now clearly audible as well as visible as the animals bleated in either fear or greeting at the approaching humans. As the group approached the flock it was clear that the goats were used to humans because they came up and mingled with them, bleating loudly and falling over each other as they vied for attention. "They must have been in one of those caves when the flash appeared" said Tom pointing over to the cluster of five or six cave entrances further up in the side of the hill. "Let's go and have a look. Maybe the owner is about somewhere too". They split up and went off exploring the caves.

A few minutes later Tom emerged from his cave and shouted for the others to join him. "Come and take a look at this" he shouted. "I've found the goatherd". They all joined him at the mouth to his cave and they all walked together into the gloomy interior. The walkway went slightly downhill for a good ten to fifteen metres and around a slight left hand bend into a small cavernous chamber that was wonderfully cool after the scorching heat of the afternoon Mediterranean sun. The ground beneath their feet was squelchy with rivulets of water that were running down the rocky walls of the cave. The daylight from the entrance some fifteen metres away, although dim cast just enough light for them to be able to see the figure of an old man curled up on his side on a small natural rocky precipice forming a bench. "Is he asleep?" whispered Manuela. "I don't know yet" whispered Tom in reply. "I'll go and try and wake him up". Tom walked over to the old man and shook him slightly. There was no response so Tom shook him a little harder. The old man's cloth cap fell from his head but there was no response. Tom felt with his fingers into the cartoid artery of the old man. There was no pulse – he was obviously dead. "I'm afraid he's dead" said Tom "but I don't think he's been dead too long. There's no decomposition at all. I don't think it's related to the flash. Maybe it's just old age or he couldn't find anything to eat or drink".

"Well it's very sad" announced Mike, not sounding a bit sad at all "but it's very lucky for us. His goats must have been in here with him when the flash occurred and they must keep coming back here to drink the water that's trickling in because they all look very healthy. I vote they now become our herd and we think of a way of transporting them to a field beside the villas. This is the start of a long term solution to our future food requirements and we need to learn about looking after goats – and breeding them". "And slaughtering them...." Hannah reminded everyone. "Yes, yes" said Mike, "and slaughtering them.....but it's something that we're going to have to learn to do. Now then – back home for a fish barbecue and then we'll return tomorrow with a truck of some kind, round them up and get them back to the fields near the villas.... agreed?"

"What about the old guy?" asked Lucy, "shouldn't we bury him?"

"No" said Mike. "He's underground anyway in this cave and there's no predators so he'll just decompose as if he were buried anyway. So, back to the villas – agreed?"

"Agreed" shouted the others and off they set back across the fields towards the vehicle, all thoughts of finding some fresh fruit and vegetables now forgotten in the wake of their most recent discovery.

The following day, Mike and Hannah were given the job of procuring enough fencing wire and the necessary tools to patch up the fencing on a field adjacent to the villas and the other three set off to find a suitable mode of transport for the goats and enough fodder for them to last a few weeks. By dinner time that evening they had there own little enclosure with 25 goats, enough hay and bagged fodder to last for ages and a brand new tin bath that was going to be used as a water supply for the goats. The self-sufficiency programme had just passed phase one and everyone was excited at the prospect of a never ending supply of fresh meat, albeit goat's meat. They agreed that they would never let the size of the herd get below twenty five, so as soon as the first kids were born they would do their first slaughtering. Hannah and Lucy also had high hopes of being able to get fresh milk and produce their own butter, yoghurt and cheese. "I never thought one of those yoghurt makers that everyone gets as a wedding present would ever be useful, but if we can find one on the island somewhere it would be brilliant" Hannah told everyone. "I think you can also make butter in them and we could even try and find an ice cream making machine too".

CHAPTER FIFTEEN

Mick Dwight stood behind the bar of the Coober Cooler (or as he put it "My pub and the best damn pub in Coober) and poured a fresh, foaming ice cold beer for everyone and as he did so he introduced Carl and Mandy to the group of locals that had decided to stay in Coober Pedy. Mick explained that over the last week or so almost everyone had left town as supplies started to run out. There had been minor instances of looting but most people had seen that no trucks were making their way into town to replenish supplies and so had headed off in various directions toward the coastal areas. Some had taken flights on the many privately owned planes but most had packed up some essentials and driven out. As far as Mick knew, the group gathered here now were the last few people in town, although he couldn't be positive about that.

The group consisted of Dave and Sandra Bullough both about fifty, deeply tanned outdoor types who owned a local general grocery store. They explained to Carl and Mandy that they had enough stock in their storeroom and freezers to keep the small group going for quite a while if necessary. Also present were Rube and Abe Goldstein – Jewish brothers who owned one of the towns many opal trading posts. Both were small men in their early forties with pasty complexions and quick, intelligent eyes and obviously brothers. The last two people at the bar were much younger than the others and spoke with an accent that was obviously European although their English was excellent. Mick introduced them as Klem and Helena Olsten. They were actually back packing around Australia and were now stuck here in Coober not knowing where to go or what to do next. As the conversation within the group grew, Carl learned that they were Danish from a small suburb on the outskirts of Copenhagen. Both were in their mid 20's and were on a gap year having both graduated from Copenhagen University with degrees in Medicine and they were delighted to hear that Mandy was pregnant.

When the initial introductions were over and the general hubbub of excited conversation had died down Carl told the whole group about his and Mandy's story and the group of friends they had left behind on Crete. They explained their hypothesis on the events that had taken place, which was pretty much the same as the Coober group had thought, even down to finding a few mutated torsos that had obviously been not quite deep enough underground to escape the full effect of the rays. Mandy took up the narrative, "we initially came because we really thought there would be a big community still here and thought that perhaps we could find a doctor. To be honest we're both a bit shocked that a town of about three and a half thousand people has all deserted in such a short space of time but we didn't realise how dependent on the outside world you were for supplies".

Mick explained, "Yeah but at the time of the flash a lot of the population would have been above ground in their houses, or working or on leisure activities. There would only have been a couple of hundred underground at the time".

Carl took over, "That explains it then. Well we promised our friends we would get back to Crete as soon as we could. The island is perfect for the situation that we're all in. There is plenty of seafood readily available, plenty of locally growing fresh fruit and vegetables and the climate is more or less perfect so we all decided that we would stay there and make it our base. The question is, do any of you feel like you might like to return there with us, pick out your own villa and make a go of it on Crete? Mandy and I are quite willing to find a larger plane and fly as many of us out of here as want to go".

Mick said, "that's a lot to take in and think about Carl mate. How about giving us a while to think it over and chat about it and let you know in the morning?"

"Yeah that's fine" replied Carl, "I wasn't expecting an immediate decision and I don't want anyone to feel pressurized. The offer's there if anyone wants to take us up on it. Right then – what about food – I don't know about anyone else but I'm starving".
"Tell you what then" piped up Sandra, "I'll cook a meal for everyone and Carl and Mandy can stay at our place tonight. Let's all go and get freshened up and meet up at our apartment in, say, an hour and a half". Everyone was in agreement and they all finished their beers and made went their separate ways. Dave and Sandra led Carl and Mandy off to a higher level to an expensive looking apartment block that was sort of built into the side of the walls of the mall. The inside reeked of money with marble and mahogany fixtures and fittings and thick plush carpets everywhere. Inside the spacious apartment that was artificially lit throughout, Carl and Mandy were given the guest bedroom and left alone to shower and freshen up after being shown where the kitchen and dining room were for when they were ready for dinner.
"They all seem like really nice people" Mandy commented to Carl as they showered and prepared. "Yes, I really liked them all" agreed Carl. "Wonder if any of them will fancy coming back to Crete with us though?"
"Well, we'll find out soon enough" said Mandy. "We'd best find out where the nearest airport of any decent size is because if any of them do want to come with us, we're going to need a much larger plane".

The evening passed very pleasantly with a beautiful meal of Kangaroo steaks in a creamy Madeira wine sauce with all the trimmings, followed by homemade Malibu and Malteser ice cream – "I know it sounds strange" defended Sandra, "but please just taste it and you will be bowled over". She was right. Mandy thought it was divine and had seconds, swiftly followed by the rest of the group who backed up her original judgment. As the wine flowed and the conversation around the table relaxed and people got to know each other Klem made the announcement "Helena and I have decided already that we would

like to return to Crete with you if that's okay Carl. We were going to move on anyway but decided that it would be foolish to try and reach Denmark. We don't think there would be many survivors there at all so Crete sounds as good a place as any to start a new life and we may be useful to the group with our limited medical knowledge".
"Well that's great news" responded Carl "and you're both most welcome".

The group split up as the girls started to clear up and the guys took glasses of wine through to the living room and relaxed in the comfortable cream leather chairs and sofas. "Anyone else made a decision yet?" enquired Carl of the group of men. Mick said that he was up for it as there was nothing left here for him now. He was a widower and a new start in a new place seemed the right thing to do in the circumstances. Dave said the he and Sandra were still thinking it over and Abe and Rube were undecided what to do because of the business. This comment absolutely astounded Carl, who thought to himself "what business do you have if there are no people left to do business with?" but he kept his thoughts to himself. He was already thinking that tomorrow he would have to fly out with someone and pick up a larger plane from the nearest airport now that it was confirmed that there would be at least five of them and possibly up to nine.

After a few more after dinner drinks, and with everyone slightly the worse for wear the group broke up and went their separate ways to bed at about three in the morning, all agreeing to meet back at Sandra and Dave's place for brunch and decision time at twelve noon the same day.

Twelve noon came and sure enough, everyone was there. Carl posed the question, even before brunch was served, "okay – has everyone made up their minds? Who's coming and who's staying?".
"We're definitely coming" said Sandra on behalf of herself and Dave.
"We've also decided to come", added Rube and Abe, almost simultaneously. "No point having a business if there's no-one to trade with, and if the state of things is as bad as you say then money is a thing of the past and it's very much back to basics I suppose".
Carl said "that's brilliant. We're going to have a proper little community and a real chance at making an excellent life for ourselves, and for this little one here", patting Mandy's tummy, "and for any other little ones that may come along in the future".
A quick plan of attack was drawn up. Carl was going to take Mick, Rube and Abe to Adelaide airport, which Mick had assured him was the closest International airport and one that would probably house the kind of plane that they were looking for. It was situated about one and a half hours flying time South West of Coober Pedy.
The others were going to sit down and draw up a list of equipment that they might need which may not be readily available on Crete and would also pack enough supplies for nine people for a return journey of three or four days duration.

Deciding not to waste anytime, Carl, Mick, Rube and Abe headed out to Coober Airfield and after about half an hour of pre-flight checks were airborne and en-route to Adelaide in the small Cessna. On the journey, Carl told the other guys all about Crete – the climate, the kind of wild food they would be able to catch or cultivate, the houses that would be available to them and he told them as much as he could about the other members of the group that were now settled there awaiting their return. None of the Australian contingent had ever been outside of Australia before, let alone to Europe so the air of excitement in the small cockpit was palpable and by the time they came to touch down at the deserted International Airport of Adelaide there was a positive feeling of camaraderie between the four men.

They taxied after landing towards the smaller terminal building that serviced the private plane sector of the airport rather than the main International terminal building. A search of the many small, privately owned planes on the hard standing came up with a mid sized, twin propeller Cessna 404 Titan Ambassador. Carl was familiar with this plane as it was the workhorse of the small executive fleet industry in the UK and all over the world. A ten-seater with good instrumentation, range and extremely easy to fly – even tough it was a twin prop.

A search through the terminal building offices again produced a set of keys for the aircraft and after some pre-flight checks Carl discovered that the tank was full and all systems were go.

"I want to take it up on my own just for a quick circuit of the airfield if you don't mind chaps" he told the others, "it will be my first time in a twin prop and I don't want to scare the shit out of you all".

Mick, Rube and Abe readily agreed that this was a good idea and stood back and watched as Carl taxied the plane away to the start of the runway, opened up the throttle and smoothly took the plane into a gentle ascent. He did a long, slow, almost lazy circuit then brought her in to a gentle touch down and taxied back to where they were all standing.

"Okay guys. No problems" said Carl "she's a dream to fly and she has a really good range so the trip back to Crete should have less fuel stops. We'll work out a route when we get back. Hop in and let's go".

They made an uneventful flight back to Coober Pedy and, as on the way out, they were all scanning the ground below them for any signs of life but didn't see a living thing for the whole journey.

Back at Dave and Sandra's apartment that evening the group who had stayed behind to recce provisions declared that they didn't think there was anything worth taking from Coober that couldn't be picked up in abandoned shops or warehouses on Crete, so they had put together a small bundle of sleeping bags, food and drinks that would see them through the journey.

Over a light supper that evening they studied aviation maps and agreed on a route home that would take them first to Rockingham to check out the naval Base and see if the survivors of the two submarines had made it back to base yet. This would mean landing at Perth and then travelling 38 kilometres Southwest by road. Once back in the air, they would fly from Perth to Jakarta in Indonesia, then to Muscat in Oman and the final leg then to Heraklion on Crete. They would allow three or four days for the trip because they didn't know how long they might end up at the submarine base HMAS Stirling at Rockingham.

They all had a relatively alcohol free evening and an early night and the next morning after a quick refueling exercise the intrepid group of new friends set off at 10AM. As the plane soared smoothly into the clear bright Australian sky they all harboured their own secret thoughts about what this new adventure and new life might hold for them.

CHAPTER SIXTEEN

The briefing of the men and officers on board HMAS Rankin had not gone as smoothly as Captain Wayne Toohey would have liked. The crew, who understandably were under a lot of pressure anyway from their enforced confinement at sea for so long, were extremely restless and there was an underlying current of disquiet and a mood of dissention. Carl would be glad when they 'put in' at HMAS Stirling in the next hour or so. He would tell the men that they were obviously released from their service and were free to go wherever they wanted. They would, he guessed, in the majority want to head to their home towns to see if there were any surviving members of their families. He regretted now telling the enlisted men during the briefing about the small colony that was being formed on Crete, especially the fact that there were women there. However, he thought to himself that no-one was going to take any notice of that when the priority immediately would be to restart some kind of sustainable life here in Australia and to hopefully seek out other Australian survivors.
In his earlier Navy career Wayne had been a helicopter pilot in the Fleet Air Arm and he was hoping to pick up one of the Navy choppers that would be at the Fleet Air Arm base in Rockingham and fly the coast line looking for signs of life. He was aware that there would have been hundreds of leisure divers underwater at the time of the flash, whatever time of night or day it would have occurred (night training dives were popular on this stretch of the coast). Also, there was a good chance that some of the navy dive team would have been out on excercises. Whatever, he thought to himself, it would be handy to have his own chopper rather than to rely on road transport once they were back ashore.

Below decks on board HMAS Rankin, in the small and oppressive 'other ranks dining mess'; a grand title for what was essentially a large table sat in the middle of torpedoes, sacks of potatoes, boxes of tinned provisions and bottled water; Ordinary Deckhand Joe Muhler was holding court with 4 other members of the crew. Muhler was a 'lifer'; he had been in the navy for 23 years and had extended his service. He had been promoted and 'bust' back down to O.D. more times than he could remember, usually because of alcohol related incidents. He was a weasel like character, thin and scrawny but deceivably muscled and strong. His tanned body (he spent most of his leave on the beach) was covered in old, faded blue and black tattoos and he had a couple of teeth missing, giving him the appearance of old sea-dog, almost piratical.
The rest of his audience were not dissimilar in appearance and represented the worst elements of the crew, easily swayed by Muhler who was in mid-flow now as he controlled the parlay with an almost mutinous narrative. "I don't care what the skipper says we should do when we land; he's released us from our service which means we can do what the fuck we want. And I say that we are not going to find any women anywhere in Australia. The continent is huge and there will only be a few hundred survivors nationwide, most of which will be blokes. You could travel for a hundred years and not bump into another living soul. No, I say that we grab ourselves the nicest looking motor cruiser that we can find and head to where we know there's gonna be women – Crete. I mean, at the end of the day we're all sailors so getting there isn't gonna be a problem is it?"

One of the other members of the group spoke up, a bald headed Aboriginal member of the crew, Wako Tamotei, his black skin glistening with sweat in the warm, humid atmosphere of the enclosed galley; "I agree mate. There's no police or anything to stop us doing what we want and this is about the continuation of the human race – almost back to the survival of the fittest if you like – and I for one don't want to live out the rest of my days somewhere where there are no women. In fact I'm going 'stir crazy' without a woman and we've only been at sea for a few weeks. Imagine spending the rest of your life without the soft touch and smell of a woman. Count me in man, Crete it is".

The rest of the small mutinous group all agreed with Muhler and Tamotei and they swore an oath between themselves agreeing to let no-one else in on the group or the plan. Once they got landside they would commandeer a vehicle, drive down to the yacht marina and claim their prize. They would look for a cruiser rather than a yacht and for something substantial that was ocean-going with a large fuel capacity. They would then spend a day or two loading it up with provisions and planning a route. They might as well make a trip of it after all, and see a few of the world's famous ports on the way. One never knew what one might bump into en-route. They all agreed that weapons and ammunition would be useful as well, just in case there was any male opposition to their plans once they reached their destination. There was no room in their plan for other males.

The small meeting was broken up by the shout 'to deck'. They were approaching HMAS Stirling in Rockingham and would be going ashore in less than half an hour now. On deck there was a sombre mood as the submarine drew into the harbour which would normally have been a hive of Naval activity. Today however there was nothing. No movement, no people, no noise – it was very spooky and the atmosphere among the forty or so men on deck was very subdued.

Once the vessel was docked and tied off, the Chief Petty Officer called the men to order so that the captain could address them. Wayne took up position in front of the ranks of men and spoke at the top of his voice so that everyone would be able to hear him.

"Okay men. This is it. In a few minutes we are all going to go our own ways, most of us I would imagine looking for loved ones. We don't know what we're going to find so I urge you all to be careful. If anyone decides that they want to come back here and start afresh I plan on making this my base for the next few weeks so I would welcome any of you. We don't know what long term effects this disaster will have on the planet – remember there is now no moon, which in the long term theoretically should have an effect on tides and weather patterns but we don't know how much of an effect or when , if at all, this would start to manifest itself. It has been a pleasure to serve with you all. I now release from your service commitments and you are free to go wherever you wish".

Wayne had expected a mad rush to get off the boat, a throwing in the air of caps and a jubilant 'hurrah'. Instead there was an indecisive milling around of bodies and a low hubbub of conversation as groups of friends gathered to discuss, now that the time had actually arrived, what they were actually going to do. There was no sign of HMAS Collins, the other sub that had been out at sea on manoeuvres at the same time as the Rankin and Wayne sincerely hoped that they were okay and had found out about the disaster and put into port somewhere. Although he planned to do sorties in a helicopter most days, he had decided to stay in the Officers Mess here at HMAS Stirling for a few weeks in case the Collins showed up or in case any of his crew decided to return. When the last of the crew had said their farewells to him and left the vessel, Wayne headed off, along with his number two, Josh Cransley towards the officer's mess. As they walked, Wayne said to Josh, "I don't know about you mate, but I feel like getting pissed tonight and starting afresh from tomorrow morning; What do you think?"

"Sounds like a plan to me mate", replied Josh, "and I'll let you know in the morning what I'm gonna do for definite but I really think I'm just gonna stay here with you".

They entered the Officers mess building at the same time as Joe Muhler, Wako Tamotei and his rag-tag bunch drove away from the dockside, all five of them crammed into a very nice looking Mercedes which one of the lads had conveniently known how to hotwire.

CHAPTER SEVENTEEN

Little Manuela awoke in her bedroom back on Crete with the morning sun streaming in through her windows and forming dancing shadows on her bedcovers. Something had woken her up; a distant noise, but she didn't know what the noise was. She walked down the grand marble stairway into the kitchen where her new adopted guardians, Tom and Lucy were sat at the kitchen table drinking coffee.

"What was that noise?" she asked as she walked sleepy eyed into the kitchen and plonked herself on Lucy's lap. "It woke me up".

"We heard it too babe" said Lucy. "Tom thinks it was a power tool of some sort. It's probably Mike starting some hare-brained Do It Yourself project. We'll have a walk over to their house later and see what he's up to".

" 'kay" mumbled Manuela around a mouthful of toast that Tom had made for her. Lucy had become quite a dab hand with the bread-making machine they had found in the house and she made two fresh, crusty loaves every day; one for them and one for Mike and Hannah. She hoped she would soon be making three a day; an extra one for Carl and Mandy. If they were true to their word they would be returning any day now and all five of them were excited at the prospect of being reunited with them and hearing about their travels.

After breakfast the three of them walked around to Mike and Lucy's villa and the source of the morning's rude awakening became apparent. Mike was in the process of turning the garden outhouse into a small dairy building. He had acquired a bank of fridges, an assortment of stainless steel and aluminium containers and receptacles and something that looked like a set of bagpipes without the sound piped in them.

He looked up from his workbench as they arrived and greeted them and told them what he was doing. So far they had been milking the goats and using the milk for everyday use as butter and cheese were still stockpiled in the house fridges and would last for a while longer.

"It's not going to be long now until we run out of butter and cheese", he explained, "so I thought I would set up a little dairy so we can make them ourselves. I've got everything I need now apart from some stuff called rennet; apparently it's essential to get the milk to start turning into cheese. That leather bag over there is for making butter – that'll be a good job for you Manuela". He pointed to the item that looked like a set of bagpipes.

"How does it work?" asked Manuela.

"Well", said Mike, "we rig it up on a framework that allows you to sit there for hours just sloshing it backwards and forwards and the milk starts to curdle and turn solid. Then you just drain off the liquid which is called buttermilk, shape the solid stuff into pats and put it into the fridge – het presto – butter; At least, I hope it's that simple. We'll find out soon enough. I should get this lot finished by the end of today".

Tom piped up, "so tomorrow should we go down to the harbour and look around for somewhere to set up our little fish farm project?"

Tom and Mike had decided to pen off an area of the harbour and to fill it with as many fish as they could catch with nets on a full day out using one of the harbours many fishing boats. Once the pen was full of fish, they could draw on those stocks for weeks, meaning that they would only have to go fishing every few months instead of every few days as they were at the moment.

They had been very busy over the few days that Carl and Mandy had been gone. They had shipped in two full large fuel tankers to supply the generators, which would keep them going for a long time. They had checked the condition of the borehole and filtration plant and it would appear that fresh water was never going to be a problem.

The three girls had taken it upon themselves to read up on goat husbandry in books pilfered from the local library and translated (loosely) by Manuela. The had even, initially started to give the goats names, but had given up when they realised that there were too many of them and that it might make it difficult when the time came for slaughter. The three of them had decided to look on it more as a business venture and were now concentrating their efforts in placing likely looking females alone with the male goats to try and induce mating.

Since the day they had found the goats, they had also found fields containing grapes, melons, cucumbers and several orchards of lemon, orange and grapefruit. They had even been to a local garden centre and taken what they needed in the way of seeds – tomatoes, peas, lettuce etc. So that they could start on their own vegetable gardens to keep the small community supplied.

All in all, they thought that they had the whole 'self-sufficiency' thing covered and both couples, after some deep late evening conversations, had decided to ditch their birth control measures and to start trying immediately for families. They were very aware that the future population of the planet could well spring from this small group and similar groups of survivors around the globe and they thought that there was no time like the present to get started – and besides, it really was no hardship!!

So things ticked over and small life preserving projects materialised and came to fruition and the group of five waited patiently for the return of their friends, each day scanning the skies and looking out for the telltale sign of a small plane coming over the island.

CHAPTER EIGHTEEN

The small passenger plane touched down at Perth International Airport pulling up just short of a Quantas jet which had ground to a halt about three quarters of the way down the main runway. Whether it was during take off or landing no-one knew, but it didn't cause a serious problem to Carl. He taxied around it and over to the main passenger terminal. They pulled up and all disembarked. Carl said to the group, "well that wasn't too bad. I suggest that we refuel now then it's ready to take off again when we return. I don't want us to spend too long here. We'll just pop down to the Naval base and see if the submarine has docked. If it has, we can have a chat with the captain and see what his plans are". Everyone agreed and Mick, Dave and Sandra were dispatched to find a suitable set of wheels for the nine of them. Abe, Rube, Klem and Helena went exploring the terminal building and Carl and Mandy set about the now familiar task of acquiring a fuel tanker and refuelling the plane. Just as they were finishing Mick came back and announced that they had a nice people carrier out at the front of the building so the three of them set off through the terminal, picking up the other four on the way who were browsing the airport shops, pocketing small items that took their fancy.

"It's funny" said Helena, "I used to get so excited at airports – you know, the shops, buying a book or a magazine, having a drink before boarding. Now, we can have any of this stuff that we want and it just doesn't bother me at all. In fact, I'm just grabbing this stuff for the sake of it. I don't need it and I don't particularly want it". This said, she put the small pile of perfume, a watch and a couple of books down on the counter and hurried along with the others out to the front of the terminal, where Dave sat in the driver's seat and Sandra in the passenger seat of a large, black Volkswagen people carrier. They all squeezed in, Sandra opened the small A-Z map book she had found in the vehicle's glove compartment and Dave rolled the vehicle around the haphazardly scattered vehicles that had stalled or ground to a halt outside the terminal.

Half an hour later they had covered the 38 kilometres to Rockingham and were driving through the suburbs looking for signs for HMAS Stirling when they spotted two vehicles heading towards them. One was a Mercedes saloon car and this was followed by a Ford Transit van. Excitedly Dave flashed his headlights at the oncoming vehicles and said to everyone, "Look guys – two vehicles. There are people here. I'm going to pull over". He pulled the vehicle over to the kerb and waited as the two oncoming vehicles approached and pulled over to the kerb directly over the other side of the carriageway from them.

CHAPTER NINETEEN

The five submariners had had a fantastic time scouring shops and warehouses in preparation for their voyage. It had taken them many hours but they now had just about everything they needed. Nautical charts and instruments, diving gear and fishing gear had been acquired from the chandlery shops down on Rockingham's elite and upmarket Marina complex. Heading inland a bit, they had found a 'cash & carry' and almost filled the transit van that they had picked up en-route with dried and canned foods and drinks, including enough alcohol to fuel a small nation. They had even grabbed a DVD player, TV and hundreds of DVDs from an electrical retailer on one of the downtown retail parks. Their next port of call had been to a builders' merchant where they had grabbed heavy duty bolt cutters, a jemmy, a sledgehammer and other bits and pieces that they thought might come in useful at their final destination - a firearms shop.

The rigid security measures at Rockingham Firearms proved no match for Muhler and his gang. Once inside they soon opened the gun cabinets and ammunition storeroom and within half an hour they were back on the road armed with an assortment of handguns, rifles and a 12-gauge shotgun complete with enough ammunition to start a small war.

Earlier in the day they had been to the Marina and while one of the gang, Gareth Crook, the youngest member of the group, scoured the chandlery shops for the charts and instruments they would need for the long voyage ahead of them, the other four had searched the marina for a suitable vessel. Gareth had been a navigator on board HMAS Rankin so, although he was the youngest of the group Muhler had put him in charge of navigation for the journey.

As he bundled his pilfered goods into the boot of the Mercedes, the other four had found the ideal cruiser for their purposes. It was 95ft Princess Gentleman's Yacht with a 10,000 litre fuel tank and a cruising range of a couple of thousand nautical miles. They clambered all over the boat, inspecting it to ensure it was up to the voyage ahead, checking the engines and the on board equipment. The fuel and water tanks were full and there were clothes scattered all over the yacht. They surmised that the owners must have been on board at the time of the phenomena that the captain had informed them all of. There were separate en-suite double cabins and the whole boat was finished in white leather and rich, polished teak.

"There's only a few hundred hours on the engines", commented Jim Parkin, the self appointed mechanic, due to the fact that he had worked in the engine room on board the Rankin. I've checked the logs and the gauges; she's practically brand bloody new mates".

" Okay, we'll would sit down later this evening, once we've finished our 'shopping' and plan a route based on how far we can get on a tank of juice", Muhler informed the other three. "That'll be the kid's department", he finished, referring to Gareth Crook. His nickname on board the submarine had been The Kid as he was one of the younger members of the crew and had a real 'babyface', barely needing to shave even though he was almost mid-twenties. "Then we'll set off tomorrow morning – no point hanging around now we've made the decision".

Now, sat in the Mercedes in the suburbs of Rockingham, stopped on the other side of the road from the people carrier, the five men looking over into the vehicle couldn't believe their luck. "I don't believe it man" said the big Aborigine, Wako Tamotei. "There are women in the vehicle too. What are we gonna do Joe?"

Thinking on his feet, Joe Muhler quickly said, "Okay, let me get out first and talk to them. I'll get them all out of the vehicle. Load a couple of those pistols quickly, and when I've got them out of the vehicle, you lot get out too. Keep them covered with the pistols and we'll take the women. Shove them in the Transit, toss the keys to the people carrier away so the men can't follow us and hotleg it down to the Marina."

"Okay mate", said Tamotei, "and once we get to the marina I suggest we put to sea straight away and worry about our route once we get going – agreed?"

They all agreed and Muhler exited the Mercedes and walked over to talk to Dave through the driver's side window of the people carrier, smiling pleasantly as he went, and calling out "G'day mate" as Dave rolled down the driver's side window.

CHAPTER TWENTY

The group of friends watched as the Mercedes and transit van pulled slowly to a halt on the other side of the highway and the driver of the Mercedes got out. He waved to them and called out "G'day mate" as he strolled behind the Mercedes and had a short conversation with the driver of the Transit van. Then he walked over to the people carrier and Dave climbed out of the driver's seat. The stranger stretched out his hand to shake Dave's and introduced himself as Joe Muhler. As this was happening Carl, Mandy, Sandra, Helena, Klem, Mick, Abe and Rube all climbed out of the people carrier and walked around to the driver's side to introduce themselves to the new arrival. When Muhler saw that they were all climbing out of the vehicle he motioned with a wave of the arm for his four comrades to come and join them. The other four submariners climbed out of the two vehicles and walked over to the small group. As they got to within a couple of yards of the group Tamotei and the fifth member of the gang, Jim Wyles both produced small pistols, pointed them at the group and Tamotei shouted, "Okay, all of you, hands up in the air – now". The small group looked at each other, at first in disbelief, Carl almost laughing as he thought it was some kind of prank.

After a second or two it became clear that it was no prank as the five men began to manhandle the group, shouting warnings to keep their hands in the air. They separated Mandy, Sandra and Helena into a separate group away from the men, with Parkin and Tamotei shoving them towards the rear of the waiting Transit van, shouting at them all the while.

Carl and the other men stood in a helpless group with their hands in the air, covered by the Muhler, Crook and Wyles with his pistol. "We're taking the ladies mates", said Muhler viciously, "and if you know what's good for you and for them you won't try and stop us or follow us – get the keys to their vehicle Gareth mate", he finished, motioning to Crook.

Crook took the vehicle keys and put them into his pocket and then said to the group of men, "Okay you lot, back into the vehicle and stay there. Don't get any fancy ideas or my mate over there with the gun will shoot you". Carl and the others, still with their hands above their heads climbed back into the people carrier and looked on helplessly as the three girls were bundled unceremoniously into the rear of the Transit van by Parkin and Tamotei, who then locked the rear door and climbed into the front of the van.

The other three walked backwards towards the Mercedes, all the time Wyles pointing the pistol at the group of men in the people carrier. When they reached the car, Tamotei climbed in the driver's seat and as soon as the other two were in, the car sped off away from the kerb, swiftly followed by the van.

In the rear of the van the three girls, although petrified, hadn't succumbed to the terror they were feeling and had remained quiet throughout the whole abduction, not wanting to antagonise the men. Now they started whispering among themselves. Helena, as the youngest was by far the most frightened. "What do you think they want with us?" she asked somewhat naively. Sandra and Mandy looked at each other with a knowing glance and Mandy replied, "No need to worry Helena – they aren't going to hurt us, that's for sure. And I'm sure Carl, Klem, Dave and the other guys won't waste anytime in coming after us. I think the best thing we can do is to just go along with them, not antagonise them and just be on the alert for a chance to get away".

In the people carrier Carl exclaimed, as the two other vehicles sped away, "Bastards – right come on guys, we've got to find another vehicle and get after them".

"Who do you think they were?" asked Klem.

"I'd put money on them being from one of those submarines", replied Dave. "Did you see the tattoos on a couple of them?"

"Whoever they are, they've messed with the wrong people", bristled Mick. "The bastards will pay for that – uncivilised bloody scum, that's what they are".

The six men climbed out of the vehicle and started down the road in the direction that the other vehicles had taken. Split into two teams, one on either side of the carriageway they made their way down the ranks of abandoned cars, looking inside them for one with the keys still in the ignition. Eventually Abe shouted out, "over here, this one's got keys in". He was stood next to an Audi A6 estate car and the others ran over and dived in. Abe took the driver's seat, gunned the car and put the automatic gear selector into drive. "What's the plan then guys. There's no use haring off after them, because even if we're lucky enough to find them, they're armed and we're not".

Carl had been thinking about this and said, "Let's head for the Naval Base as we originally planned. If the captain of the submarine is about I'm sure he'll help us, plus, they will have an armoury there with lots of weapons in it".

They all agreed that his was a good idea and Abe set off following signposts for HMAS Stirling as the angry conversation in the car speculated on what they were going to do when they found the men who had abducted their women. Although no-one said anything, the underlying fear was the time factor because they were all fairly positive that rape was the main purpose of the abduction. As they approached the Naval Base there was a broody silence in the car as each of the men harboured their own thoughts.

There was no guard on the gates of the base and the whole dock area appeared to be deserted. They parked the Audi and climbed out. There was a distant noise which they all recognised as the sound of helicopter blades. It was coming from the rear of the large barrack building on the edge of the parade square, so the six men edged carefully around the building towards the noise, taking care not to be seen by whoever was at the helicopter just in case it was the abductors.

As they reached the final edge of the building, Carl peeked around the corner and saw a small two seater helicopter, blades spinning, stood on the centre of a small helipad. There was one man in the cockpit, helmet on, clipboard in his hands. He looked like he was performing pre-flight checks. Carl said to the others, "Okay guys. You lot stay here. I'll run over and see who it is. If it looks like I'm in trouble – get over there quickly and help me out". The others all grimly nodded their assent and Carl dashed out from the cover of the building and sprinted the sixty or so metres to the waiting helicopter and rattled on the side of the Perspex cockpit.

CHAPTER TWENTY ONE

Captain Wayne Toohey had awoken with a blazing headache and a mouth like the bottom of a budgie's cage. He and his number two, Josh Cransley had polished off several beers and the best part of a bottle of Jack Daniels the previous evening and despite several glasses of water and a couple of Nurofen, he still felt delicate. Josh had agreed to spend the day sorting out enough rations for them for an extended stay at the barracks and was also trying to sort out a generator so that they would have some power in their section of the Officer's Mess for as long as they decided to stay there.

Carl had found one of the small navy Black Hawk?? helicopters on the helipad and he was now in full flying rig, hangover almost dissipated, finalising his pre-flight checks. He was going to do a rotary sweep of Rockingham and surrounding areas to see if there was any sign of life.

He finished his checks and reached over to put down his clipboard when he spotted movement out of the corner of his eye. There was a man running towards the chopper, hunched over to avoid the whirling blades and gesticulating to him. Carl did not recognise him as one of his crew members and was instantly wary. He hit the 'kill' button and the engines died. The blades started to slow and the man approached the cockpit. Wayne opened the small thick Perspex door, removed his helmet and stepped away from the chopper motioning to Carl to do the same. They walked twenty or thirty metres away so that they could hear each other above the diminishing noise of the rotor blades. Carl introduced himself, reminding Wayne of the radio conversation he had had with Mandy a few days previously. He then proceeded to tell him their tale since that radio conversation, ending with the abduction of the girls.

"Christ", said Wayne "I think I know who a couple of those guys will be from your description and I could take a guess at the others as well. Right Carl, what do you suggest we do first?"

Carl replied, "Well I didn't realise you'd have access to a helicopter. Would it be okay if we got up in it straight away and did a sweep of the area to see if there's any movement anywhere – either by road or by sea. I think time is of the essence. It's my wife out there and.............well, she's..........", Carl faltered slightly as tears began to well up in his eyes. He loved Mandy dearly and the tears were tears of anger as well as despair. He would kill any man that hurt her. " She's pregnant with our first child", he continued.

By now, Klem, Mick, Abe, Dave and Rube had joined them and Carl made the introductions all round then Wayne spoke to the group.

"Okay guys – here's a plan. We'll go over to the armoury and find my number two – Josh Cransley – and he'll kit you guys out with a weapon each. I suggest that you and he then head down to the marina area in case these guys decide to go seabound. Carl and I will take the chopper up and check out the area for any signs of movement either on land or at sea. We'll grab a couple of two way radios from the stores as well so that we can stay in touch".

Everyone agreed that it was as good a plan as any and they set off to find Josh Cransley. Forty five minutes later Carl and Wayne were in the air and the six other men were in the people carrier heading for the marina. Each man carried a browning 9mm pistol and Josh Cransley had equipped himself with a Steyr Australian issue rifle fitted with a telescopic sight and two magazines of 5.56mm rounds. Josh had shown each man how the pistol worked, how to load, make safe and unload and where the safety catch was. The agreement was that they would only use them if there was a life threatening incident or confrontation.

Carl and Wayne scanned the area above Rockingham in a standard box pattern search but didn't see a thing except the people carrier with the others in it heading for the marina. They started the search well inland and were slowly making their way back towards the ocean. As their search reached the shore Carl spotted something out at sea about two miles away; a small white dot on the horizon.

"What's that over there?" he spoke into his headset microphone to Wayne, pointing out to see to indicate where he meant. Wayne acknowledged that he had seen it and swung the chopper out to sea to investigate. As they approached they could see that it was a very large, white and blue motor cruiser travelling at quite a speed heading out to sea.

"I'm going to go lower so we can take a look", said Wayne into his headset, banking the chopper down to the left and swooping in low over the fly deck of the motor yacht. As they made their pass Wayne could see clearly that the person at the helm was an aborigine and he recognised him immediately as one of his crew members, Wako Tamotei. As confirmation that they had found the group, two other figures emerged on deck at the sound of the helicopter. Wayne recognised Joe Muhler and Jim Parkin straight away.

"Well, we've found them and they're a bad bunch right enough. They must have the women below decks. We'll head back to base and meet up with the others. I think I know how we can sort this out" Wayne said to Carl. He then got on the two way radio to Josh and informed them of what they had found. He told Josh to get the Naval Launch ready to put to sea and they would meet them down by the launch very soon.

He explained his plan to Carl as they headed the chopper back to HMAS Stirling. The other six men would head out to sea in the Naval launch which had a faster turn of speed than the motor yacht. Carl and Wayne would pick up the yacht again in the chopper and track it, directing the launch in towards it. As the launch neared the yacht, they would fire from the chopper tear gas grenades from a rifle with an under slung grenade launcher from the chopper into the yacht. This would incapacitate everyone on the yacht so that Josh and the rest of the guys, who would be wearing NBC gas masks, could board and over power the five men and rescue the girls. It all sounded good to Carl as they landed the chopper and trotted off to the stores to pick up the gas masks, grenade launcher and a handful of tear gas grenades. They put the grenade launcher and grenades into the chopper and headed down to where the launch was idling at the dockside with the six other men milling around preparing it for sea.

Wayne outlined his plan a second time for everyone. They checked that the two way radios were fully charged. Wayne gave them the gas masks and they watched as the launch pulled away from the dockside. Carl and Wayne headed back to the chopper and were soon heading back out to open sea in search of the yacht.

CHAPTER TWENTY TWO

Joe Muhler could hear a faint buzzing noise above the noise of the smooth engines of the powerful yacht. He thought nothing of it at first and was distracted as Tomotei brought him up a cold bottle of beer from the galley. They had loaded the stores onto the yacht very quickly at the Marina and set off to open water straight away. The women were locked up in one of the cabins below decks and the rest of the guys were below playing cards watching over the women.

There was a bit of a race on now as Tomotei had told Muhler that he'd overheard another group of lads from the crew of the Rankin talking among themselves. They too had a plan to grab an ocean going boat from the marina and head towards the island of Crete. Muhler had no idea if they had left already or not but he was taking no chances and wanted to put as much distance as possible between themselves and the western coast of Australia as soon as possible.

There was that buzzing noise again, only getting louder this time. He looked around to see what it was and Tomotei hit him on the arm and shouted, "Up there mate – a bloody helicopter – look".

Muhler looked up just in time to see a Black Hawk?? Helicopter swoop down and buzz the fly deck of the yacht.

"That looks like one of the choppers from the base mate", said Tamotei.

"Yeah and it looks like it was the captain flying the bugger too", replied Muhler. "Surely he can't have found out about the women already can he?"

Tamotei said, "Well I heard him saying he was hanging around base looking for survivors. Maybe he just saw the boat and wanted to check it out. Now he's seen us he might just go away – in fact look – he's heading off back to shore now".

"Okay", said Muhler, "that's probably all it was. Not much he could do anyway though mate. Do me a favour will you? Take the wheel while I go and check everything's okay down below".

Tamotei took the wheel and Muhler went below decks to use the heads and to check how the guys were doing.

In the small cabin Sandra, Mandy and Helena were sat on the double bed. Helena had been sobbing uncontrollably realising the situation they were in and aware of the likelihood of what was to come on a voyage that looked like it would last at least a few weeks. They had racked their brains to try and think of a way out of their situation or of a way to let someone know what had happened to them but they were in an impossible situation. The best they had come up with was to throw themselves overboard at the earliest opportunity but this would only be any use if they could do it without being spotted other wise the yacht would just turn around and they'd be picked up again.

"The problem with throwing yourself overboard though", pointed out Sandra, "is that there are sharks in these waters for a start, and secondly you might bob around for the rest of your life out there because there's no-one around to pick you up any more".

Mandy said, "I'm sure that Carl and the rest of the guys will find us. They know that these guys are sailors and will suspect that they'll head out to sea. Carl can fly planes as we know so he'll come looking for us – I'm sure of it. We've just got to hold on until they come for us. I think the main thing is......if these guys want to....you know....use us", she glanced at Helena who gave her a weak smile and said, "I know what you mean – don't worry about me – I'll be fine – I'll kill anyone who tries to touch me".

"Well I was going to recommend just the opposite", said Mandy. "Just play passive – go along with it. Just lie there and say and do nothing. Don't antagonise them. Hopefully they'll get tired of it if we just treat it as something that has to be done and we remain emotionless. Don't speak to them or give them any feedback at all. Basically let's just act like rag dolls".

"I agree", said Sandra, "Don't give the bastards the satisfaction. Although I do think that if we get the chance to injure or kill one of them then we should take it. We're a very valuable commodity and I don't think they have any plans to kill us or even hurt us".

As they finished the conversation, Helena said to the other two, "listen, what's that noise?" She reached over to crane her neck and look out of the small porthole on the side of the cabin. "A helicopter", she screeched with joy, "you were right Mandy. Carl has come looking for us already".

"Well it won't be Carl", said Mandy. "He can only fly fixed wing aircraft, but I do think it's a good sign and they must have found someone to come looking for us".

A few minutes passed during which the girls chatted about the possibilities of what the helicopter's appearance might bring, then, suddenly the door to the cabin burst open and Muhler stuck his head through the door. "Don't get any ideas of freedom from the helicopter ladies. Just our old captain making a routine flight looking for survivors we reckon. You're all ours now and as soon as we get well underway we're gonna have us all a great party", he laughed wickedly and winked at the girls then pulled the door shut, locking it again from the outside.

The girls cowered on the bed again whispering among themselves. Up in the saloon Muhler told Crook, Parkin and Wyles that they would get well out to sea and set the autopilot then they could make a start on the booze and 'introduce' themselves to the ladies. They all laughed at that, spirits high and Muhler went back up to the fly deck and told Tamotei the same thing.

CHAPTER TWENTY THREE

Up in the black hawk Carl and Wayne had both the Navy launch and the yacht a few miles ahead of it, in their sights. The launch was capable of a good 10 knots more than the yacht so it was gradually closing the gap. Wayne was keeping the chopper well back so as not to alert the gang on the yacht.

On board the launch Josh Cransley ran over the plan again with Rube, Abe, Mick, Klem and Dave and had a re-run of the weapons brief he had given them earlier. They were all quite grim faced and serious looking as the realisation of what they were about to do was sinking in. None of the men on the launch had ever taken a human life and each one secretly prayed that this situation didn't get so out of control that this would change.

Up in the chopper Carl checked and double checked his rifle and grenades. The rifle was loaded already with the first grenade. They were going to try and get as many grenades into the yacht as possible from the chopper before the launch finally did its final approach and the other guys boarded the yacht.

After what seemed a lifetime to Carl he saw that the launch had gradually drawn to within a few hundred metres of the yacht and he saw it visibly slow down as Josh eased back on the throttle. Josh asked for a situation report over the two way radio and Carl informed him that, from where they were a few hundred metres off the stern of the yacht, he could see no sign of life on the fly deck and he assumed they were all below. Carl knew that the yacht would be fitted with a very sophisticated autopilot system and there was a good chance the gang had activated this while they were below decks.

"Are you ready for action then mate?", asked Wayne.

"As I'll ever be", replied Carl.

"Okay, inform Josh we're going in now and he can start his approach", said Wayne as he banked the chopper.

Carl told Josh over the two way radio that they were beginning their part of the operation. Josh gunned the throttle and the launch picked up speed and started gaining on the yacht over the last few hundred metres. Carl slipped the safety catch off on the rifle. There was still no sign of life on the fly deck as Wayne brought the chopper in close to the rear of the yacht. They were going to fire one grenade into the saloon from the rear then try to get one into the cabins on the port and starboard side. Only about 50 metres away now and Carl brought the rifle up to his shoulder, took aim and pulled the trigger.

In the saloon of the yacht the sound system was cranked up to full notch blasting out The Beautiful South song 'Rotterdam' and all the men had cold bottles of beer or large glasses of spirits. There was a definite party atmosphere and the five men were having fun and savouring with anticipation the moment when they would get the women out and the party could really start.

Suddenly there was a shattering of glass as something came flying through the double glass doors that separated the saloon from the fly deck. This was followed by a small bang then a hissing noise as the first grenade detonated and the noxious tear gas chemicals began to flood the room.

"Jesus Christ", shouted Muhler, "that's tear gas". A couple of seconds later another grenade entered the saloon in the galley area and the room was thick with the acrid, burning chemicals and smoke. All five of the men had tears streaming from their eyes which were now shut tight against the invading chemicals, rendering them virtually blind. Rivulets of thick snot streamed from their nostrils and within a few seconds all of them were rendered helpless on the floor, vomiting and gagging on the fumes. The third grenade crashed through a porthole in the master en-suite cabin further forward, but was totally redundant as that cabin was empty and the five men were already incapacitated.

After a minute or two, as they tried to crawl their way blindly over broken glass to the outside, Dave, Klem and Josh entered the cabin with their gas masks on, weapons pointing at the five pathetic figures huddled on the floor. Rube was maintaining a watch on the launch, keeping it alongside the yacht and Abe was on the fly deck waiting to see if anyone made a break for it.

Josh and Dave made their way around the spluttering gang members one at a time, binding their wrists behind their backs with strong black cable ties that they had brought along especially for the job.

Klem commented, in a muffled voice through the thick rubber and glass face plate of his gas mask, "No sign of the girls. I'll look for them while you get these out of here and onto the launch".

Josh nodded his approval and he started dragging the men one at a time out onto the deck while Mick covered the remainder with his weapon. Out on deck, he knocked off the autopilot and brought the yacht to a halt. Rube did the same with the launch and tied it off to the yacht. They began to drag the men out one at a time and hauled them across onto the deck of the launch where they were instructed to lie flat on their faces and not move otherwise they would be shot.

As this was happening, Klem had located the cabin where the girls were sitting. They had been petrified when they heard the glass shattering and the explosions. They were affected only slightly by the small amount of gas that had crept in under the cabin door, so Klem told them to stay put for a few minutes until the worst of it had cleared and closed the door on them once again.

Eventually all five gang members were bound and lying face down, still coughing and spluttering on the deck of the launch. Very subdued and in no mood to fight or struggle, they had been easy victims of a well executed plan and Josh was pleased with how things had gone. He informed the chopper that all was under control and he would see them back at base.

Josh, Abe, Mick and Rube kept the gang covered on the launch while Dave and Klem, after waiting a few minutes for the air to clear, released the girls from the cabin. There were hugs and kisses all round and Mandy was only slightly disappointed to find that Carl wasn't here.

It was decided that Josh, Abe, Mick and Rube would take the launch with the prisoners back to base and Dave and Klem would follow in the yacht with the girls. The chopper veered off and headed back to shore, followed by the launch and the yacht. All the men were secretly very pleased with themselves that the plan had worked a treat without a shot being fired. But each one of them without exception also harboured doubts about what to do next. There was no justice or penal system. What would they do with the five men? How could they punish them in such a way that they would no longer be a threat to anyone in the future?

CHAPTER TWENTY FOUR

Back on Crete, Tom, Lucy, Mike, Hanna and Manuela stood on the quayside of the small fishing village and peered into the bright morning sunlight, cocking their heads to try and better pick up the faint droning sound that they could all hear. They had been fishing and swimming and generally having a lazy Mediterranean morning when Manuela had alerted them all to the distant drone of an engine. At first only Manuela's young ears had picked up the almost imperceptible noise but gradually the older members of the group also registered the sound.

"Maybe it's Carl and Mandy" said Manuela, "it sounds like an aeroplane to me". The others waited a moment or two and each agreed that it did indeed sound like an aeroplane. "I can't see anything", said Hanna excitedly, "but it definitely sounds like an aeroplane to me. It's got to be Carl and Mandy. Come on, let's head out to the airport and see."

They quickly packed up their fishing gear, picnic basket and towels and headed back to the car. They bundled in unceremoniously and headed off to the airport, chatting excitedly between themselves, speculating as to whether or not it was Carl and Mandy, whether or not they would have anyone with them or if they would have brought back anything exciting with them.

It had been over three weeks since their friends had departed and although they had achieved a lot towards making their new homes and lifestyles sustainable in the new world that they had built for themselves, they had all secretly missed Carl and Mandy and, more importantly longed for news of the possibility of other survivors of the natural disaster that had occurred for which they still had no reasonable explanation.

As they neared the airport all of them were scouring the skies and eventually Tom spotted the small aeroplane as it made its approach into Kefalonia airport. "There it is", he shouted, pointing out the aircraft to the others. "It doesn't look like Carl and Mandy though. The plane is too big – look it's got two propellers and it's got more windows that the small one they left here in".

"Well it must be them", reasoned Lucy. "Maybe they've swapped planes or something. It's too much of a coincidence that someone else would choose to land here of all places, isn't it?"

Everyone agreed that it was and Mike pointed out that they would find out in a couple of minutes as they were now approaching the airport and the plane, which now actually didn't look so small, was just about to touch down.

The big BMW sped across the tarmac to the now stationary plane just as it was discharging its gaggle of passengers onto the warm tarmac. As they heard the car engine Carl, Mandy and their new friends from Australia turned towards the noise. Carl and Mandy waved excitedly and Mandy ran towards the vehicle as it pulled to a stop a few yards away from the plane. Everyone got out of the vehicle and there was lots of excited hugging, kissing, back slapping and handshaking as the seven friends became reacquainted with one another. While all this was going on, the group of newcomers, Mick, Dave, Sandra, Abe, Rube, Klem & Helena all stood awkwardly around waiting to be introduced. Finally, Carl and Mandy brought the two groups together and noisy introductions were made all round in a general atmosphere of relief and happiness that everyone was safe and sound on both sides.
Everyone was keen to hear the news from the other group and to find out about the newcomers but Carl called a halt to the proceedings as the noise level was reaching such proportions with everyone talking excitedly over each other, that they could barely hear each other.
He suggested that they hijack another vehicle, pick up the one they had left at the airport and get all fourteen of them back to the villas where they could organise some sleeping arrangements for the newcomers, sort out some food and settle down to swap stories of what each other had been up to since they were parted.
Tom and Lucy volunteered to host a 'bit of a do' around the swimming pool, offering to fire up a barbecue if the others could sort out some accommodation for the Australian contingent.
They all agreed this was a great plan and after the procurement of an additional vehicle from the front of the terminal building, all three vehicles with their compliment of happy survivors headed back to the beautiful part of the island that they had decided upon as home for the foreseeable future.

Four hours later they were all sat around the swimming pool tables with a plateful of barbecued goat meat, fish and shellfish and several bottles of wine and cold beer (and coke for Manuela) as Carl began to recount the turn of events as best he could recollect from the past three weeks since he and Mandy had left Crete in the little plane; although it felt more like three months than three weeks.

Everyone listened in awe as he told of the kidnap and rescue operation and finished off the story with incarceration of the five kidnappers in the naval prison under the watchful eyes of their other new friends, Wayne and Josh.

CHAPTER TWENTY FOUR

"Well what's going to happen to them then?" asked Lucy breathlessly after a short silence at the end of Carl's story.

"We're not sure" replied Carl. "The two Naval officers that we told you about, Wayne and Josh, just said that they would deal with the kidnappers appropriately and then helped us to get everything together to head back here. They said they would deal with the situation there and they would follow on by boat to meet us here as soon as they possibly could. We didn't ask any questions and here we are. They reckon they should be with us in five weeks or so. We told them whereabouts on the island they could find us and they said they would bring as many trustworthy individuals as they could find with them when they came. Most of the crew of the submarine had vanished to try and trace relatives and friends that may have survived in various other parts of Australia but there were signs that some of them were still in the vicinity".

Between Tom and Mike the tale of the building of a small sustainable community was told. The small fish farm, the goat herd and the dairy were major success stories and the group started formulating plans for a small area to grow crops, which although still abundant at the minute would soon have to be properly farmed if they were to be readily available for future seasons. A couple of the Aussies volunteered to try and set up some sort of smokery so that they could preserve fish and meat to provide variety in their diet and a couple of the girls vowed to spend a few days plundering the island's deserted retail outlets for interesting foods and drinks that had long shelf lives. These could all be stored in buildings near to the residential area that they had established for themselves so that people could just help themselves as and when they needed anything.

The evening progressed into a happy affair with lots of splashing about in the pool. Much wine and beer was drunk and it was a very content gang of fourteen people that made their way to their various established or temporary bedrooms in the early hours of the following morning, some of them a bit the worse for wear than others but all of them incredibly happy to be alive and to be with other survivors that they could class as friends. The need to be part of a group in adverse conditions such as had been thrust on them was becoming obvious to all of them, and it was true that there was safety and security in numbers.

The following day was mostly spent helping the new Australian members (and the Danes, Klem and Helena) to find their own villas and vehicles and Manuela made it her business to check out each one and give it her seal of approval whilst at the same time securing from each one of them an assurance that she could 'sleep over' at any of the houses when ever she wanted to.

Carl called a meeting of all of the men that evening whist the girls prepared an evening meal for everyone at Carl and Mandy's house. He wanted to discuss the security issues surrounding the fact that a full submarine full of sailors now knew that there was a settlement of survivors, which included several women, fully established on the Greek island of Crete.

"My concerns are that they are experienced sailors who will probably not find any female survivors in Australia with it being such a huge country. They could search for years and even if there were survivors, they might never stumble across them. They have it in their ability to pick up a large ocean going boat and make their way here within a few weeks. They could come fully armed and …….well, we saw what happened with five of them who hadn't had female company for a few weeks whilst they had been at sea…..so what would a larger group be capable of? I suggest that we take some measures, just in case." There was a general hubbub of agreement and Mick piped up, "what exactly are you thinking of mate?"

"Well, first of all we have to stay put for five or six weeks", replied Carl, "because I fully expect Wayne and Josh to turn up. While we wait for them I suggest that we all find some firearms and train everyone how to use them and ensure that we carry them with us at all times just in case. I also think, once Wayne and Josh turn up, that we could consider moving from this island to another location somewhere else nearby in the Mediterranean just in case there is a group of hostile submariners that decide to come looking for us".

"Where would you suggest we move to that's far enough away so that they wouldn't stand a chance of finding us if they come looking?" asked Abe. "We don't know this part of the world at all so we're going to have to be completely guided by you". Carl thought about it for a moment or two and then replied "I was thinking of the island of Cyprus. It's not too far away, it's Mediterranean so it has a similar climate to here, it's a larger island so we may find more survivors and it has a more diverse flora and fauna because it also has a large mountain called Troudos where it snows through the winter months".

At this point Dave chipped in, "Well I don't think we should move at all. You guys have got a great set up here with the generators, the houses all grouped together, the herd of goats which could possibly be the only other land based mammals left on the planet for all we know. Also you've built the little fish farm which is nearly fully stocked now and the butter and cheese from the dairy is brilliant. I think it would be folly to give it all up just in case we can't get a similar setup sorted out if we move somewhere else".

A few of the other guys nodded in assent and Carl said, "okay then, we'll stay put for now but I still think we should look for firearms and train everyone up on them". Everyone agreed with this and the meeting was called to a halt and the guys all trooped over to Carl and Mandy's kitchen with impeccable timing as the smell of freshly baked bread and a steaming cauldron of goat meat curry drifted through the open patio doors. The entire group spent another pleasant evening dining and drinking and formulating plans for the next few days.

It was agreed that Carl and Mick would be responsible for finding a weapons supplier on the island and acquiring enough guns and ammunition for everyone and for training everyone on how to safely use them.

The two brothers, Abe and Rube were assigned the task of going out on a fishing boat with nets to catch enough fish to finish off the stocking of the small fish farm. They also agreed to try and get a small shellfish farm sorted out if they could find an abundant supply of mussels and oysters. In fact, they said that they would spend a few days sailing around the coastline because there was a chance that a commercial shellfish farm already existed somewhere off the island.

Mick, Dave and Sandra accepted responsibility for farming duties and said they would find a few fields locally that looked arable and work out a series of easy to manage crops that could be planted and grown on a cycle that would supply them with some kind of fresh fruit and vegetables all year round. It was taken for granted that there would always be an abundant supply of things like oranges, lemons, grapes, olives etc. as these were plants that more or less managed themselves and grew very well year after year without human intervention.

Tom, Lucy and Manuela agreed to carry on with the milking of the goats and looking after the herd as well as keeping the supply of butter and cheese flowing from the small dairy on their property. It was agreed that from now on they would only butcher a goat when a new kid had been born. This would help to sustain the level of milk and to ensure that there was always enough meat in reserve for emergencies.

The two Danes, Klem and Helena along with Mandy, Mike and Hannah decided that they would spend several days scouring the island for all manner of food and drink supplies that had a long enough shelf life to be worth bringing back and storing. They would be looking for canned and dried goods, soft drinks and alcohol, bulk items such as flour, sugar, tea, coffee, rice, pasta and anything else that looked useful such as charcoal, firelighters, matches, insect repellents, fishing equipment and anything else that took their fancy. It would all be stored in one of the houses that were still empty and each household could then help themselves to whatever they needed whenever they needed it.

The next day the work began and over the ensuing few days the small community gradually built up a solid foundation of supplies and procedures that would fare them well over the coming months and years. Carl was pleased with the way things were taking shape and with the way everyone seemed to have bonded but always preying on his mind was the possibility of a boatload of sailors heading their way from Australia. As the days wore on he took it upon himself to keep a vigil on the local quayside and almost daily went there armed with his fishing tackle, but also armed with a 12-bore shotgun, several rounds of ammunition and a powerful pair of binoculars. As much as he was looking out for trouble, he was also looking out for telltale signs of the arrival of Wayne and Josh who he still believed would show up in the coming days or weeks.

CHAPTER TWENTY FIVE

The warm Mediterranean weeks drifted happily and somewhat lazily into months. Mandy was fast approaching the nine month point in her pregnancy and was absolutely huge. Carl often commented that he thought she was surely carrying more than one baby, yet she had come through the pregnancy looking the picture of blooming good health and radiant as every mother to be should. There had been no complications and with an expected delivery date that was now only days away, everyone in the group was very excited.

There had been talk among the group on the subject of procreation, given that their small group, as far as they knew, could harbour the few remaining females on the planet. As a result, Tom and Lucy, Mike and Hannah and Klem and Helena had all been trying for a baby over the last few months and all three of the girls were now in various early stages of pregnancy. Dave and Sandra had been cajoled by the others to also start a new family but had stuck to their guns, insisting that they were far too old and would instead lend a hand with all of the other children when they arrived.

Lucy who had been a nurse in what the all now referred to as their 'former lives', had been scouring the island for books in English on the subject of gynaecology and child birth. She informed the rest of the group that she was as ready as she would ever be for the birth of Mandy's first child. Lucy and Mandy had even turned one of the spare rooms in Carl and Mandy's villa into a makeshift delivery room and had taken every item they could possible need for the delivery from the local hospital. Mandy had been very insistent on the nitrous oxide and the ready prepared injection capsules of pethadene that they had found. As she pointed out to Lucy – "I'm not scared really but there's no point in being in pain if I don't need to". Lucy agreed wholeheartedly with her, secretly thinking that when her time came in a few months, she too would seek the aid of every painkilling item they could lay their hands on.

As the group awaited the arrival of Mandy's first labour pains, most days would find the men sat on the local jetty with their fishing tackle and a cool box full of chilled beers. The discussions invariably always drifted back to the topic of the consequences of the loss of the moon on the planet. It was an area of total speculation, although they had all read up on the subject. They all agreed that the scientists who had written the books and articles they had read, although undoubtedly brilliant in their fields, were just guessing at what would happen. They, however, in the course of the next few weeks, months or even years, were going to find out for themselves firsthand what the results of no longer having a moon were going to be. As yet there had been no noticeable change in weather patterns, winds, levels of the sea or other tangible evidence that anything drastic was imminent.

Their major concerns were the repercussions if the earth did actually begin to speed up on its axis or if the angle of its axis changed slightly without the gravitational pull of the moon to keep it in check. Would it make it harder to walk? Would there be more or less gravitational pull? If it began to spin too fast would it cause hurricanes? Would they go flying off the earth's surface into outer space? No-one new the answers so all they could do was talk about it and wait for the first signs of anything unusual beginning to happen.

It was mid-afternoon on a warm mid-February day while Carl and Mike were the only ones out on the jetty fishing and enjoying a cold beer, discussing the usual topics when Carl suddenly held his hand up to Mike and gestured for him to be quiet.
"What's up?" asked Mike.
"Listen", replied Carl. "Can't you hear it? A faint humming noise."
Mike listened intently. With no background noise of vehicles, birds twittering or any of the other hundreds of everyday noises that would normally assault the eardrums, the day was very still and very quiet….but….yes, there it was. A faint humming noise coming from somewhere off shore and getting louder. "I hear it now", said Mike. "It's coming from offshore. Could be a boat or a plane maybe".
They both stood up and peered out to sea, blocking out the glare of the sun with the palms of their hands. "I can't see anything", said Carl "but I've got some binoculars in the fishing bag". He reached out and picked up the binoculars, put them to his eyes, adjusted the focus and began to scour the horizon. All of a sudden he froze. "Oh my god

Mike, it's a boat. I can just make it out probably a couple of kilometres out and it's heading this way".

"It could very well be Wayne and Josh you know. After all, they were professional naval officers and they gave us their assurance that they would eventually find us".

I'm sure it is them", agreed Carl, "but let's check the guns and make sure they're fully loaded and working just in case eh? Also, get on the radio to the other guys and get them down here sharpish with some extra weapons"

The whole group, with the exception of little Manuela had taken to carrying a loaded sidearm with them at all times just exactly for this eventuality. They each also carried mid-range duplex two-way radios with a range of ten kilometres so that each member of the group was always contactable. They were all too painfully aware that if a boat did show up one day, it was just as likely to contain a small contingent of mutinous submariners from Australia as it was their friends, the officers Wayne Toohey and Josh Cransley.

It only took five minutes before the squeal of tyres and brakes signalled the arrival of Dave, Klem, Abe, Rube, Tom and Mick in the 4x4. They bundled out of the overpacked vehicle and trudged to the end of the jetty with an assortment of weapons and ammunition to join Carl and Mike. The boat was now clearly visible and the engine could be heard quite clearly. Through the binoculars Carl confirmed that it was flying an Australian ensign and it was a very large, modern ocean going power yacht. He thought to himself that, back in the day, it would have cost somewhere in the several million dollar bracket and smiled inwardly to himself at how little that meant now. One could just help oneself to any item, however expensive, as long as it was there for the taking.

The cruiser was now very close and the group could make out two figures on the fly deck. Carl held the binoculars up to his eyes once again and confirmed, "Yes it's them – it's Wayne and Josh". As he spoke the two figures on the fly deck began waving and the whole of the shore based group waved back excitedly. Eventually the cruiser pulled up to the side of the jetty, ropes were thrown and secured and the two Australian submariners jumped down onto the jetty. There was much back slapping and shaking of hands, followed by the opening of several cans of beer and lots of chattering as everyone talked over each other in their excitement.

Carl calmed things down and suggested that, before the new arrivals related the tales of what had befallen them since they had last met, they should all go back up to the villas to join the girls. Abe and Rube said they would drive back and pick up another vehicle first as they would not all fit in the 4 x 4, especially with some of the gear that Wane and Josh had brought with them. By the time all of the fishing tackle was packed away and Wayne and Josh's equipment was unloaded from the cruiser, Abe and Rube had returned in two vehicles and the group loaded up and set off back to the villas.

The greetings and hugs and kisses from the women brought a smile from ear to ear to the faces of Wayne and Josh and when the introductions and hullabaloo had died down and temporary living space had been found for them, Wayne said, "Right then, if someone gets the barbecue on, we'll tell you what we've been up to. We haven't had proper food for weeks".

CHAPTER TWENTY SIX

Around the swimming pool at Carl and Mandy's villa, the barbecue was issuing forth delicious smells of char grilled goat steaks and fresh fish straight from the Mediterranean. The entire group were sat or stood around the tables that were sagging under the weight of fresh food, breads and cold drinks and the centre of attention were the two new arrivals.

Josh took up the narrative. "Okay, where do I begin?" he said. "After you guys left us we had the bad guys locked up for a few days in the cells in the old Naval Police guardroom on the base. After a few days we realised it was going to be impossible to hold them indefinitely because we just didn't have the resources and manpower to hold them. We wanted to begin our voyage here to meet up with you guys. We had to feed them, allow them use of the toilets and showers and to be honest it was a pain. We knew we were going to have to let them go so we started to get our vessel provisioned and fuelled and ready for the voyage. Then we bundled them all, still handcuffed into a van and drove them out of town into the bush about fifteen miles. This would give us plenty of time to get away and would mean that they could get back to town within four or five hours and not be a danger to us. We set off a good few weeks ago and have made our way slowly here, visiting some interesting places on the way and at the same time looking out for any other survivors".

"Did you find anyone else?" asked Carl. "No mate, we didn't", replied Josh, "but we have picked up some interesting longwave broadcasts on some of the hi-tech maritime radio equipment we managed to bring with us. There are survivors out there and we have tuned into at least two different groups who are sending out a permanent looped message on longwave frequencies. One of these groups is based in Paris and appears to be made up of hundreds of motorists who were in vehicles in Paris's network of city tunnels at the time of the occurrence and passengers on the Metro system – at least that's the gist of what I understood with my knowledge of French. The other group is based in Nottingham in England and appears to be made up of nearly all men from different small coal mining communities"

Tom spoke up, "You know, there must be thousands of small, isolated pockets of people just like this all over the world. People stuck in tunnels, miners, divers, metro and underground railway passengers in most of the world's big cities. I think we're okay, I think the human race is going to be fine. It's going to take a long time to rebuild things to the way they were but there must be people of all professions and trades dotted all over the globe".

Wayne spoke this time. "One thing we did notice on our journey was a slight change in weather and tide patterns. Generally the winds for this time of year in the areas we have visited have been slightly stronger than we would usually expect. Also, in all of the ports we have visited the sea levels have been extremely high. It won't have been apparent to you here because you're in the Mediterranean where there are no tides anyway, but everywhere we've been there have been no discernible tide patterns at all. I think we can expect an increased change in weather patterns because of the lack of a moon. I also read some speculation that we can expect the cycle of day and night to be thrown out of kilter as well, with the duration of light and dark gradually decreasing making a complete day much shorter. That doesn't really bother us because we no longer live our lives by the clock but it would be interesting to monitor it and catalogue each day from sunrise to sunset and just see if a pattern is developing".

"Good idea", agreed Carl. I also read that one of the expected results of the lack of tides and disrupted weather patterns was for widespread flooding but I think the risk of that here is quite minimal because we're in the Med and also, the villas we have chosen are uphill quite a bit above sea level. I think it would be prudent to build some sort of fortified storm shelter, perhaps - underground possibly. We could provision it so that we could all be safe inside it for a long period of time - just to be on the safe side".

Mick piped up, "We've been thinking about something like that for a while now. Rube, Abe and I talked about this just a few days ago. We will start on that project if you like once we find a suitable location. We want it near the villas so that we can all reach it fairly quickly in case of an emergency".

Mandy suddenly stood up, knocking over a bottle of wine as she did so. "Guys, I don't want to worry anyone but I think my waters have just broken" she said.

CHAPTER TWENTY SEVEN

It was the calm after the storm. All the guests had gone and it was just Carl and Mandy in the bedroom. Mandy in bed holding the newly arrived and absolutely gorgeous Jessica Amy and Carl sat at the side of the bed with that 'ear to ear' grin synonymous with first time new dads.
The birth had been a breeze and had lasted only three hours. However, the aftermath of the celebrations, which lasted some five or six hours was now apparent all over the bedroom. Littered champagne bottles and beer cans were everywhere. Mandy had drifted in and out of sleep clutching the baby, while everyone else hovered around her cooing and clucking and enjoying the party atmosphere of a very impromptu 'baby's head wetting'.
"I'm glad they've all finally gone", said Carl. "I'm really tired now and you must be exhausted".
"I am", replied Mandy, "but it was special and I didn't mind them all being here after she arrived. I thought Lucy did a great job and I was dead chuffed that I only needed nitrous oxide – good stuff that by the way".

Carl got into bed and they put baby Jessica in between them. Within minutes the new family of three were fast asleep.

Over in Mike and Lucy's house the party was still in full swing. The excitement of the arrival of the two Aussie officers and the new baby seemed to have given everyone a real moral boost and everyone was chatting excitedly about the new baby, the Aussies journey and about what future plans the group should have. Towards the end of the party, there were just the single guys left talking around the kitchen table, half empty beer bottles aplenty and speech beginning to get a bit slurry. Now that there were no women present the topic of conversation had turned to just that subject – women- or rather, the lack of them available here for the single guys.

The subject was debated for quite a while and the outcome was that Wayne, Josh, Mick, Abe and Rube would talk to the rest of the group about the possibility of heading out on an expedition to mainland northern Europe or even the UK to try and evaluate what life would be like for the group in a different location where there were a lot more people in the community. They would broach the subject the next day, stressing that it would definitely only be a reconnaissance trip, with all of them heading back to Crete afterwards to report on their findings before any of them made any final decisions.

"After all lads", said Abe as the meeting broke up for the night and they all went their separate ways to bed, "there has to be loads of single women out there somewhere for all of us, and as much as I like you guys, I don't want to spend the rest of my life living with you in celibacy".

That agreed, they all tottered off drunkenly to bed.

CHAPTER TWENTY EIGHT

Nobody surfaced much before noon the following day and as the early afternoon sun got hotter people drifted in slowly from their own villas to the swimming pool area at Carl and Mandy's place. Mandy was holding court and breast feeding Jessica, Manuela was splashing around in the pool with Hannah, Lucy and Helena and the rest of the group were sat around the tables chatting amicably.

Rube turned to Carl and whispered to him, "Carl, me, Abe, Josh, Wayne and Mick want to have a word with everyone about a plan we are thinking about. Is this a good time do you think?"

"It's as good a time as any", replied Carl. "What's on your minds?"

"Well, I'll let Josh and Wayne take the floor if you don't mind, because they would have a better idea of what would be involved if it's all agreed", said Rube who then shouted over to the two Australians, "Hey Wayne, Josh....get everyone assembled and let's discuss what we were talking about last night. See if we can't bash out a plan between us all".

With that, Josh shouted everyone up and there was a hushed expectant silence around the table as Wayne took control of the impromptu meeting.

"Last night", he began, "the five of us single guys got to talking about......how can I put this delicately.....? well, we miss having a woman of our own and, as much as we love it here, we decided that we would like to go exploring a bit further afield to see if we can find any groups like ourselves that have any single women in the group. We wanted to suggest that we went on an initial reconnaissance trip to somewhere in Europe to have a look at a couple of major cities and see what the situation was like. We would only want to make it a short trip initially to get the lay of the land and then to report back here to everyone on what we find. We can take a small plane from the airport rather than going by sea and we would hopefully be back within a few days, just the five of us – me, Josh, Abe, Rube and Mick. Any comments anyone?"

There was a short silence then Dave and Sandra both piped up, almost in unison, "what will you do if you find anyone?"

Wayne replied, "well we would come back here, report what we have found to you guys and then we could all discuss what the next step would be. In a perfect world, for me anyway, it would be to find a woman that wanted to be with me and eventually convince her to come back here to Crete with me and join our little group. I don't particularly want to move permanently to another part of the world, however, if I find someone and she doesn't want to relocate, then I can't say I would rule it out".

The discussions rocked back and forth for an hour or more and in the end it was decided that the five single guys would set off in a couple of days time in the twin engine from the airport and would do a recce of Paris and London on a trip that was to last no more than a fortnight. Before they left they would rig up a long wave radio receiver set to a pre-set frequency on which they would make regular updates from whatever location they were in so that the group back on Crete knew where they were and what they had found. It was also decided that they would travel armed with handguns, hidden away in their clothing as a stand by safeguard in case they found themselves in a situation that demanded the use of force. They did not want to appear at first sight to anyone they would meet, to be aggressive, which is why they decided to hide the firearms.

With the meeting over Abe, Rube, Mick, Josh and Wayne dived into one of the 4 x 4s and headed out to the airport to check out the twin engine and refuel it ready for the flight. They decided that they would leave the day after tomorrow, which would give them time to get together any gear they decided they wanted to take with them. It was decided that the remaining members of the group would not start on any new projects while they were away in case those projects turned out to be futile because the recce party had found something or somewhere far better than their current situation. Mandy was particularly keen for their expedition to be over as quickly as possible because she and Carl had decided that they wanted everyone in the group (including young Manuela) to be sworn in as Godparents to little baby Jessica in an ad hoc ceremony that she would work on while they were away.

Two days later, the small huddle of survivors stood on the tarmac at Heraklion airport shielding their eyes against the glare of the early morning sun as the small plane with it's manifest of five single guys and a few pieces of kit headed slowly upwards and out over the brilliant blue waters of the Mediterranean on the first leg or it's journey to Paris. Each had their own thoughts about what they would like the guys to find but for the next two weeks all they could do was wait and check out the radio set for incoming messages every 6 hours whenever it was possible for the guys to transmit at midday, six in the evening, midnight and six in the morning. Wayne and Carl had synchronised their watches so that someone was definitely listening at the correct times for each transmission.

CHAPTER TWENTY NINE

The small plane touched down without incident at Paris Charles de Gaulle airport. During the flight the five friends had seen no sign of life or activity either on land or at sea. The group carried their kit the few hundred yards from the tarmac to the front of the airport where they hijacked a Porsche Cayenne that still had fuel in it and with the keys still in the ignition. They drove as far as they could into the city until the roads became too clogged with stalled and abandoned traffic to carry on. They hunted around and within twenty minutes they had found five mopeds and scooters and were once more on their way, swerving around any obstacles as they went.

They headed in single file towards the Arc de Triumph at the top of the Champs Elysees and, as they rode, each one of them was amazed at the ghostly silence and eeriness of a major capital city in total silence apart from the tinny reverberations of the five small motorcycles. They decided to try and find something to eat and sit down to sort out some kind of plan to maximise their search. They found a small, local store down a side street just next to a small hotel proudly boasting itself as Hotel Du Bois. They grabbed a few tins of food, wrinkling their noses at the smell of the once fresh produce that had been in the store that had now decayed beyond recognition. They then retreated to the foyer of Hotel Du Bois and sat around a table in reception opening their tins. Josh wandered off to the bar area and returned with a couple of bottles of red wine and they all tucked in in comparative silence, tired after the flight and the drive from the airport.

After their meal they decided that they would grab a few hours sleep in the hotel bedrooms and start their search of the city later on foot so that they would be alert to any sounds that they might otherwise miss if they were on the noisy motorcycles. They each found a room that had not been slept in since it was last serviced and agreed that they would meet back in reception in four hours time. They did not actually put a time to it because in reality none of them actually knew exactly what time it was in Paris at that precise moment in time, although Wayne did make them all synchronise their watches with his. It was decided that they would unpack the small long wave radio transmitter and make their first broadcast at midnight just to keep the rest of the gang back on Crete up to speed with what was happening.

A few hours later, Wayne opened his eyes, feeling very groggy and wondering what the noise was that had woken him. He looked around the unfamiliar room, trying to remember where he was and saw the watch on the bedside table realising that it was the alarm that he had set before he'd climbed thankfully in between the lovely, cool, crisp white cotton sheets of the hotel's king size bed. He got up, showered and brushed his teeth, got dressed and went with his small kit bag down to the reception area where they had agreed to meet up. Josh, Rube and Abe were already there sat in the lobby waiting, all looking suitably refreshed and scrubbed. "No sign of Mick yet?" asked Wayne. "No mate", replied Josh, "we'll give him five minutes and then we'll go and look for him in case he's overslept. Anyone see what room he went into?" Nobody had noted which room Mick had slept in, so after five minutes, when he still had not turned up, they all went off down the ground floor corridor looking for him. Rube found Mick's small kit bag in room 126 but there was no sign of Mick. The bed in the room had not been slept in either and Mick's bag was still packed. Rube called the other three who all came running to the room. "Bloody hell, where the hell is he", asked Wayne. "His bed hasn't even been slept in. Let's carry on searching in case he found another room but forgot to take his bag with him. Josh and I will take the first floor. Rube, you and Abe take the top floor. Meet you back down here in a few minutes". They split into their teams and went off to their respective floors to carry on the search. Fifteen minutes later they were all back in reception having found no sign of the larger than life Australian ex-Mayor of Coober Pedy. "I reckon he mustn't have been tired and went walkabout and has just lost track of time" said Wayne, "let's give him half an hour and if he isn't back, we'll leave him a note and meet him back here again this evening. I think we should look around for some walkie talkies though and keep one with us at all times so that nothing like this happens again. We'll look for some as soon as we set off in half an hour".

Half an hour passed and there was still no sign of Mick. The group left the hotel, turned right onto the small side street that brought them out on to the Champs Elysees and turned right heading in towards the city centre. The skyline ahead of them was very impressive with the imposing structure of the Eifel Tower in the background. They kept their eyes peeled for a small shop that would stock walkie talkies and after about half a mile they found a small electrical shop that stocked mobile phones, radios and all manner of electrical gadgets down a small cul de sac. They grabbed five handsets and filled a small carrier bag with the correct batteries. They fired up the radio sets, tuned each one into the same frequency and tested them out. They worked fine and they agreed that whatever happened, for the rest of this trip, they would keep them on their person and turned on at all times. The sets boasted a range of ten kilometres which they all agreed was very impressive. They all filled their pockets with spare batteries and resumed their course down the wide tree lined avenue, past the now silent and lifeless designer shops and luxury car showrooms, the Disney Store and the inescapable MacDonald's, which was giving off a particularly nasty odour. "Probably all the burgers rotting in the freezers", pointed out Abe as they all wrinkled their noses and hurried onwards past the restaurant.

They scoured the city for a few hours but with no success. They were all aware of a distant background noise – like a dull, continuous throbbing – somewhere off in the distance but each time they tried to trace it they had no luck. The sound seemed to surround them, very low in volume but appearing to come from every direction and its exact source could not be located. After a few hours they were tired and hungry so it was agreed that they would head back to the hotel and get something to eat. They could also make their first broadcast back to the rest of the group in Crete who, they were sure, would be standing by the radio in anticipation at midnight. As they wearily crashed through the hotel doors, Mick greeted them with a cold bottle of beer in his hand. "I managed to find a little portable generator", he explained gesturing towards the hotel kitchen."Loaded the fridge up with beers for you guys. Thought you might be thirsty". "Where the hell did you get to?" asked Josh. "We were worried about you". Mick replied, "get yourselves a beer mate and I'll tell you all about my day. It's been very interesting".

They all grabbed a cold beer and settled into the chairs in the hotel lobby. Mick continued, "After you all went to bed I knew I wouldn't be able to sleep so I went out to explore the area. Well, I've never been to Paris before! Anyway, I lost all track of time and I lost all track of exactly where I was. In other words I got lost. Anyway, everywhere I went I could here this deep humming noise and as I walked further it got louder and louder, so I followed the noise. I ended up getting close to the Louvre and I'm pretty sure that's where the noise was coming from. I reckon it was a bank of generators and I swear I could hear peoples voices coming from the Louvre as well but I didn't want to explore any further on my own, just in case there were people there and they weren't very friendly".

"That would make sense", said Wayne. "The Louvre is a huge museum and it's mostly underground. I bet there are people living there, underground, not wanting to risk being above ground for too long in case there's a repetition of the flare. How did you find your way back Mick?"

"I remembered the name of the hotel and the street and I found a little tourist shopping stall with maps of the city. I didn't realise that I had walked so far", replied Mick.

"Well I think that's worth further investigation tomorrow morning then, don't you guys?" asked Wayne. The other four agreed that it was and the rest of the evening was spent opening tins of food, drinking beer and formulating a plan for the morning. At midnight they radioed a short situation report back to Crete and then hit their beds, agreeing a rendezvous of eight o'clock the following morning in reception.

CHAPTER THIRTY

After a breakfast of cold water from the fridge and some vacuum packed 'long-life' croissants one of them had found deep in the hotel larders, the gang of five loaded up their weapons and walkie talkies and set off on a direct route for the Louvre. It was decided that Wayne, Josh and Mick would hang back and cover the situation from high up in a nearby building, while the two brothers, Abe and Rube approached the main glass pyramid entrance structure of the Louvre on foot with their weapons and walkie talkies concealed. If anything untoward should happen, Wayne, Josh and Mick would be in a good position to react from their vantage point. The group was silent as they made their way towards the deep thrumming noise that definitely got louder as they approached the general area of the Louvre. When they were one block away they could tell that it was definitely the sound of several large generators working together. They could also hear the sound of laughter, possibly children. They were very excited but also cautious now at this stage.

They found a rear entrance to a tall administration building that had a frontage onto the square that housed the glass pyramid. They worked their way up to the second floor and found an office at the front of the building that had a good vantage point of the entrance and concessions stalls of the Louvre. As they looked out of the window, amazingly, they could see a group of five adults and a handful of children in the square. The children were playing with a beach ball and the adults were sat in a group chatting. The scene did not look threatening at all and there was no sign of weapons. Abe and Rube decided it was time to approach the group. They went back out of the building by the rear entrance and walked around the side of it, quite openly into the main square.

The group of children were the first to see them approach. All laughter dried up and they stopped playing with the ball and just stood open mouthed watching as the two strangers approached. The group of adults noticed them a second or two later and the group stood to their feet.

From the window on the second floor across the square the other three guys watched with interest. There was no sign of any aggression or fear on the part of the group of adults or children; just an air of curiosity. "Maybe they get stragglers turning up all the time", remarked Wayne, "after all it is a huge city and a huge country".

Abe and Rube walked directly up to the group of five adults. There were two men and three women. Abe shouted out "Bonjour" as they approached and Rube said "Ca va?" "Ca va bien", replied one of the men as he walked towards them, arm outstretched for a handshake.

They all shook hands and gave their names but it was apparent within seconds that the two brothers' knowledge of French had been exhausted. One of the French guys, Luc, switched to fluent English as soon as he realised that Abe and Rube spoke English. "You have come from England?" he asked them. "No, we're Australian", replied Rube. "It's a long story - but we have some more friends over in that building. Is it okay if they come over?" Luc nodded his assent and explained in French to the rest of the group what was happening. Abe sent a message over the walkie talkies and the other three made their way into the square. The children surrounded the group as the adults all introduced each other in broken English and French. After a few moments Luc said to the five new arrivals, "come, I will take you inside and show you where we all live and we can talk". He led the way into the magnificent glass structure of the Pyramid, down a number of flights of stairs and down a procession of well lit passageways into a main atrium, which had been transformed into a huge dining area with tables, chairs and all the accoutrements of a nice restaurant, including candelabra, clean white cotton table cloths, fine china and cutlery. Somewhere there was the fabulous smell of food cooking, with a hint of garlic in the air. On their way to the dining area they passed several small individual chambers that had once housed art collections from a particular artist or from a particular period in time that had now been turned into extravagant living quarters, furnished with the finest Parisian furniture, pictures and ornaments – thanks to the opulent collections of the Louvre.

As they were ushered into chairs around a large round dining table the five friends looked at each other and smiled. This set-up made their humble abodes on Crete look positively peasant-like. Wine was served, plates of nibbles appeared and both groups began the lengthy process of telling their individual stories. A few hours later it was apparent that, although the French had a fantastic life here, it was now a community of mainly couples with adopted children. Abe, Rube, Mick, Wayne and Josh hade been perfectly honest about the reason for their journey from Crete and the French group were totally sympathetic. They had explained that most of the single males that had been here at one time had gone off on similar quests themselves, albeit without the benefit of aeroplanes. They indicated that most of them had headed for the coastal resorts on the southern Mediterranean shores of France. They also advised against travelling to other large cities because they had a feeling that it would be a similar story wherever they went. The five friends, although buoyed by their meeting with the French group, were disappointed but were given a glimmer of hope by an elderly dapper gentleman who spoke only in French but was translated by Luc. He told an enchanting tale of his younger days when he was a French Naval officer on board a French Naval Frigate in the 1950's sailing the Japanese pacific outlying islands.

He told of whole communities of women called 'Ama', who lived with their children in small, isolated coastal villages, separate from their men folk. The men lived in communities inland and farmed crops, cattle, goats and pigs. Some of the Ama specialised in free diving for wild, natural oysters on secretly guarded beds rich in natural pearl bearing oysters. Others dived for Conch, with its rich white meat and others dived for sea cucumber or sea urchin. The women were the main family breadwinners and would spend months in the seaside villages free diving up to forty times a day for dive periods on a single breath sometimes in excess of two minutes at a time. Surely, he hypothesised; there would have been hundreds of these women underwater at the time of the phenomenon.

Josh and Wayne had also heard of these people. They had cruised those waters for years with the Australian Navy and were now kicking themselves for not remembering about the Ama earlier.

Everyone chatted a bit longer, hypothesising about how many women there might be and how their ages must surely be younger rather than older due to the extreme physical nature of their occupation. Eventually the five friends decided they would take their leave and head back to the Hotel du Bois. Their new French friends pleaded with them to stay, have dinner and spend the night at the Louvre but the friends had made up their minds that they would travel back to Heraklion the following day. They bade farewell to their new friends, giving them detailed information of how they could be found on Crete if any of them ever ventured in that direction, and made their way back to the hotel.

After a quick radio check back to the gang on Crete, they all turned in for the night ready for an early flight back to the Mediterranean island that they now called home, albeit temporarily.

CHAPTER THIRTY ONE

Manuela shrieked excitedly, jumping up and down shielding her eyes from the bright mid-afternoon sun as the small plane began its descent. "Here they are, here they are", she shouted, pointing to the small plane. The rest of the small group had all turned up at the airport to greet the five guys when they returned. Everyone had spotted the plane and there was an excited, expectant chatter between them all.

The plane landed and taxied over to where the small group huddled on the airport apron at the end of the taxiway. The five guys stepped down from the cramped passenger compartment and there were hugs, kisses and handshakes all round and lots of excited greetings and questions. Eventually the hullabaloo died down, everyone headed back to the vehicles and they all made their way back to the villas. It was agreed that everyone would meet at Carl and Mandy's swimming pool that evening at six o'clock, giving the five guys time to get sorted out and have a couple of hours rest.

Hannah, Lucy, Mandy, Helena and Sandra all set to in Mandy's kitchen; there was bread to bake, wine and beer to chill, salads and fruit to prepare and there was an excited, party atmosphere in the kitchen as the girls worked. Manuela was given small jobs to keep her occupied and Mike, Carl and Tom went off to choose a mature goat that could be slaughtered for the barbecue that evening. Dave and Klem volunteered to head down to the fish farm and bring back a few fresh fish to compliment the meat, while the five adventurers headed off to their own villas to stow their gear and get their heads down for a few hours prior to the evening festivities.

At six o'clock they all met at the pool. Some of the guys had already started grilling huge steaks of goat meat and whole, fresh silver Mediterranean fish (none of which anyone could name). A few of the group were swimming and some of the girls were ferrying food and drink out from the kitchen to the outdoor tables. There was a carnival atmosphere and an overall feeling of relief that the five guys had made it back to the island safely and without incident. Secretly, every member of the group that had stayed behind on the island were desperate to hear the story of the guys' trip but everyone was happy to wait until they had all eaten their fill and had a few drinks.

Eventually the meal was finished and everyone sat around in a circle around the tables. Carl had piled the barbecue high with logs and there was a wonderful campfire throwing flames up into the cooling evening air and throwing off a lovely warm glow to those sat near to it.

Wayne took up the narrative and told the complete story of their trip from start to finish, prompted by the other four if he missed any part of the story out. Before the conversation could get too heavily involved with the next step of the "guys' quest for women", as Carl had light heartedly labelled it, he interjected with a comment of his own.

"Well we have had our own little bit of excitement while you have been away", he said. "Tell us more", replied Wayne. "Sounds interesting".

"Well, I was fishing one day from the jetty down at the marina when I spotted a large boat, quite a way out to sea. Through the binoculars I could just make out the Australian ensign flying from her rigging. Naturally, we feared the worst and immediately thought of those Australian seamen of yours finding their way here, because it was inadvertently leaked to them that this is where we had made our base. Since then we have kept a low profile and watched the shoreline steadily but have not had another sighting of them. I think they are still out there though. It's a big island with a huge shoreline, so I am sure they are looking for a sign as to where we might be. I think we need to come up with a contingency plan of some kind….just in case".

Wayne replied, "well that scuppers part two of my proposals, which would have been to equip ourselves as soon as possible and set off on a recce of the Japanese islands. They will already have seen the plane landing this morning so they will know that we are here somewhere. It's only a matter of time before they stumble across us. Perhaps we should be pro-active and go on the offensive. Anybody got any ideas?"

The rest of the night was spent discussing the trip to Paris and formulating a plan to tackle the new, serious threat posed by the sighting of the motor cruiser. If it was indeed the submariners from Australia, and everyone agreed that it must be, then the danger was very serious. The group decided that the best form of defence was attack and a plan was struck to lure the seaman into an ambush.

Tomorrow mid morning they would pick a strategic spot that would be good for an ambush and light a fire with green brushwood that would give off lots of smoke. The women would stay at the villas and the men would man the ambush ground with automatic weapons.

"And what exactly are you going to do with your automatic weapons once you have these guys in the ambush ground?" questioned Mandy, who had now got to her feet and was standing facing Carl and Wayne with her hands on her hips.

Carl and Wayne looked at each other and a few of the other guys looked away or looked down at the ground.

"Er.......well.......we have to kill them Mandy", replied Carl. "We have no choice. You can bet that if they find us first they will certainly kill at least all of the men and do god knows what to the women".

"I'm afraid he's right Mandy", said Wayne. "I've worked with these guys and they're not pleasant people at the best of times. They are going to be very pissed off at what we did to them back in Australia plus they have had no female companionship for months now. They are very dangerous and threaten our existence here".

Eventually the discussions petered out and the guys all went off to check their weapons and ammunition. The girls all went back to their respective homes and there was a sombre note in the air as they all said their goodnights to each other.

CHAPTER THIRTY TWO

The following morning saw all of the men out of bed and gathered at the garage at Carl's house where most of the weapons and ammunition was stored. The group of ten men loaded up three vehicles with the weapons, ammunition, food, water, binoculars and other bits and pieces they would need. As Wayne had pointed out, it could be a long wait and might not even be productive. Only time would tell. Once loaded up they all dived into their vehicles and headed towards an old dried up river bed that ran inland from a small estuary about ten kilometres south of their current location. Klem and Helena had spotted this spot on a picnic previously and Klem had told the guys that he thought it would make a great spot for an ambush if they could lead the seamen up the river bed from the shore. About half a kilometre inland the walls of rock and scrub rose on either side of the river bed and there were ample places to hide.

They reached the spot and drove the four wheel drive vehicles inland staying parallel to the riverbed but not so close that the tracks left by the vehicles would be spotted. About a kilometre in they found a perfect place to hide the vehicles in an abandoned, tumbledown barn built of old grey stone. It had no roof and the walls were crumbling but it was a high enough structure to hide the vehicles.

They unloaded all of their gear and made their way across the scrub to the high canyon walls alongside the river bed. Wayne sent Rube off, armed with a couple of axes, to find firewood, with instructions to particularly gather stuff that looked as if it would throw off a lot of smoke.

He then organised the rest of them into four teams of two and positioned them with their weapons, ammo, food and water in strategic places, well hidden by rocks and gorse thickets, either side of the river bed. As he positioned each team he gave them the same instructions.

"Stay alert guys. Keep your weapons locked and loaded with the safety catch off. Also, keep your walkie talkies on channel twenty six and I'll keep you appraised of what is happening. If they come I'm pretty sure they will approach from the shore because they will be using the boat to look out for signs of us. Nobody shoot until I do. I will be further down the trail with Abe, towards the shore so I will see them first and I will know when they are all in the kill zone. When you hear my first shot, open fire and make every shot count. I've placed you all in spots where you will not be cross firing into one another. Good luck guys".

As he placed the last team in position he saw that Rube had managed to light the fire and smoke was billowing forth already. There was a clear blue cloudless sky and the smoke must have been visible for miles. As Rube got back to where Wayne was situated he had second thoughts about the positioning of everyone and said to him, "New plan Rube. You had better stay by the fire and keep putting stuff on it as the day goes on otherwise we might give away our positions by moving every time it needs topping up".

Rube agreed that this was a good idea, took his weapon and supplies and trotted off to the fire while Abe and Wayne made their way further upstream to their vantage point. Wayne had picked his spot carefully so that he could also see the coast and would therefore know if their plan had worked and where the boat had put ashore.

Wayne did a quick radio check with the others and they all settled in for what could be a long, hot day under the burning Mediterranean sun.

They didn't have to wait long. Within two hours Wayne spotted the large cruiser rounding the headland from the north and going at a fair old speed if the size of the wake was anything to go by. He radioed the others to appraise them of the situation and then settled back to see if it was just coincidence or if the crew of the boat had actually seen the smoke from their fire. Half an hour later and he had his answer; the boat had pulled in as close to the beach and the estuary as it possibly could and had anchored up. Wayne watched through his binoculars as several members of the crew fitted the small outboard motor to the inflatable dinghy aboard the cruiser and launched it to the stern. Although they were too far away to make out individual faces, Wayne counted about fifteen people and, although he couldn't be absolutely positive, he thought that some of them looked like women. "Maybe this won't be what we thought it was going to be", he said to Abe after he had told him what he was seeing. He relayed these facts to the other groups by radio and told them all to stand by.

He trained his binoculars back onto the cruiser and saw that the small inflatable dinghy was now heading towards the sandy shore with a crew of about five or six people. Several of the others had stripped down to swimming costumes and had dived in and were now swimming towards the shore. As they all got closer, Wayne could clearly see that there was a mixture of men and women and that they were unarmed. In fact, far from appearing threatening, as the group all gathered on the shore they appeared to be in high, jovial spirits and Wayne and Abe could hear them laughing and shouting among themselves. Once the group had pulled the small inflatable onto the golden sands of the beach they all started to walk up the dry, cracked river bed towards where the five different groups were hidden in the bushes and rocks, weapons loaded and ready to go.

When they were only about two hundred metres away Wayne could make out the facial features of the group. He recognised immediately the craggy features of some of his old submarine crew and leading the group was the wiry, muscular ringleader, Joe Muhler. He was dressed only in swimming trunks and Wayne could make out the tattoos covering his tanned, muscled arms. They were getting so close now that he could even make out the black gaps in his teeth as he laughed where there would once have been teeth, probably long since knocked out in countless bar-room brawls in different ports all over the world.

"Submariners truly are a breed apart", whispered Wayne to Abe, smiling to himself and relaxing slightly as he noted that none of the group fast approaching their position was armed. He got on the radio to the others and informed them that as soon as the group reached the small group of boulders underneath an olive tree about seventy metres ahead of them, everyone was to stand up and shout "halt". This position would put the group, which he could now see consisted of seven guys and seven women, roughly in the middle of all of their current positions. Wayne then told everyone that he would go down and talk to them and the rest were to keep him covered with their weapons until he radioed them with further instructions. "If anything goes 'tits up' and it looks in any way like I am in danger, then open up on the bastards", was his closing transmission.

Less than two minutes later the group reached the olive tree, and almost as a single entity, Mick, Dave, Josh, Carl, Klem, Tom, Mike and Rube all stood up, pointing their weapons down at the group of men and women and shouted in unison, "HALT!"

At the same time Wayne scrambled down through the scree, rocks and gorse bushes and landed in the river bed about twenty metres behind the group. They all had stood in stunned silence when they heard the shout of 'halt' and watched in amazement Wayne's slow progress down the side of the gorge. Nobody had made a move and, although the laughter and conversation had dried up, there still did not appear to be anything threatening at all about the group.

Wayne walked towards the group along the crunchy, arid surface of the riverbed and as he did so, Joe Muhler turned to face him and started walking towards him, smiling, hand outstretched offering a handshake. Wayne stopped a metre away from him, ignoring the outstretched hand. There was a short silence, then Muhler dropped his hand, wiped it as if it were somehow dirty, on the front of his shorts and, still smiling said, "G'day skipper. Howzit going?"

CHAPTER THIRTY THREE

"You've got a bloody nerve Muhler", Said Wayne through clenched teeth. "What the fuck do you think you're playing at turning up here like this? You're bloody lucky we didn't shoot the lot of you on sight".

Muhler took Wayne gently by the elbow and steered him away from the rest of his group, just out of earshot. There was a shout from Rube up on the hill. "Everything okay down there Wayne?" In response, Wayne told the rest of his group up on the canyon sides that he was just going to have a little chat with Muhler and there was nothing to worry about. Everyone should come on down onto the riverbed but stay on alert.

About ten metres away now from the main group of men and women that had accompanied him from the cruiser, Muhler turned to Wayne and said, "Look Skipper. You're quite right. We deserve to be shot after what we did in Oz a few months back and you would've been quite within your rights. We're all pretty ashamed of what we did and we haven't come here to cause trouble. In fact, quite the opposite. We're hoping that once you hear our story and meet everyone in our new little group, you might agree to let us stay and start afresh here with your lot. I know we don't deserve it but we have changed a lot in these last few months and we thought it would be good for both of our groups to integrate".

Wayne replied, "Okay Muhler, start talking. I recognise some of the lads from the sub but who are the rest of these people?"

Muhler explained, "Well, after we managed to get back to civilisation when you dropped us off in the bush – good move by the way – took us bleeding hours to get back to town – well, we decided we would head to Sydney. We were sure there would be lots of people about just because of the sheer size of the city and of the population. Anyway, we'd been in the city a couple of days, scouting around looking for signs of life without success. On the third night there we were all walking down what would have been a busy main street at one time, can't remember exactly where, but it was near the university. Anyway, bugger me if one of the small pub/hotels wasn't all lit up with music blaring out. This lot had set up base there, rigged up a load of generators and were celebrating somebody's birthday when we stumbled in on them. Gave them the shock of their lives I can tell you". He turned back to face the rest of his group, gestured to them with a flourish of his right arm, with a comical half-bow and said, "Captain Wayne Toohey. May I introduce you to the remaining members of the University of Sydney Caving and Potholing Association? No need to ask how they all survived I assume?" he chuckled.

By this time, the rest of Wayne's group had scrambled down the canyon sides. Wayne told them all to unload their weapons while he decided what to do next.

"Skipper", whispered Muhler, interrupting Wayne's train of thought. "Some of these guys are pretty bright – University lecturers, students and the like. That guy over there is a doctor specialising in trauma surgery and a lecturer in medicine. It might be a good idea to listen to their theories about what happened and what we can expect to happen in the future. Especially that lady over there", he gestured towards an attractive blond, suntanned lady that Wayne guessed was mid to late thirties and about five feet ten inches tall with curves in all the right places.

Muhler gestured her and the doctor over and introduced Wayne to them. Her name was Leslie Dorfman and she was a professor and lecturer in Astronomy and Astral Physics at Sydney University. Or at least, as she was quick to point out, she used to be. She was very attractive and Wayne was instantly smitten by her, holding on to her hand after the handshake just a little longer than was absolutely necessary. The doctor was introduced as Matt Payne and had a strong firm handshake. He was tall and a bit overweight but looked like a powerful guy. Wayne liked him immediately.

Wayne excused himself for a few seconds and moved away then to join the other nine members of his group. He filled them in briefly on what he knew so far and said that he thought they were genuine. He suggested that they go back to the others up at the villas, have a meeting and discuss the situation, then meet up later with Muhler's group to discuss things further if everyone agreed. They would not give away the location of their villas at this stage and they could come back later on and meet Muhler's group on the cruiser. They all agreed with this plan and Wayne told Muhler what they proposed. He told him to keep the cruiser moored up where he was for now and some of them would come back down to the cruiser in a few hours time for further talks. He discovered that the group was now seventeen people strong made up of the five submariners from the original group and twelve members of the caving club; nine women and three men. Muhler was quick to point out that only three of the women were now in relationships with three of the original submariners.

The groups split up and headed off their own separate ways with hesitant goodbyes. Wayne's head was spinning with the information he had absorbed and trying to decide if it was a safe situation or if there was still an element of danger here. His instincts told him that Muhler was genuine and that the situation was exactly as described by Muhler and that it was safe to proceed with further talks as long as the rest of the group agreed. The ten of them reached the vehicles, stowed all of their gear and drove back to the villas. They called everyone to Carl and Mandy's house for a meeting to discuss the events of the day so far.

CHAPTER THIRTY FOUR

The discussions went on all afternoon around the pool at Chez Rutherford. The women were understandably hesitant because of the kidnapping and violence back in Australia all those months ago, as were a couple of the guys. After much debate however, the final consensus was that they would give the new group a trial period so that each member of the group could make an informed decision as to whether or not the intruders should be allowed to join their society. This would all be done by meeting them on neutral ground for the first few occasions so as not to give away their home locations. Wayne re-assured them that the new additions to the submariner's group all looked like decent responsible people and he was sure that the five wayward submariners had turned over a new leaf. He also pointed out that the doctor with them could be quite useful bearing in mind that Lucy, Hannah and Helena were all due to give birth over the next two to three months. At around five o'clock that afternoon Wayne, Carl and Josh drove down to the marina and climbed into a small speedboat they had commandeered a few months previously for getting around on fishing and diving trips. They headed around the coast to where the huge cruiser lay at anchor. As they approached, they all noticed that it was an impressive vessel – a Princess Motor Yacht – and it looked to be around eighty to ninety feet long. It was a superb craft and must have cost millions of dollars back in the day. Right now though, it was host to a gang of swimsuit clad people catching the late afternoon sun, drinking sundowners on the aft deck. Some of the group were swimming in the clear blue waters. A shout went up as the speedboat was spotted and all the swimmers clambered aboard. The speedboat drew alongside the cruiser and the mooring ropes were thrown aboard, made secure and the three guys climbed aboard amid greetings, introductions and handshakes.

After the introductions and when everybody was gathered on the aft deck with a cold drink in hand, Carl spoke on behalf of the three of them.

"Welcome, all of you, to Crete. There are a group of seventeen of us now that have decided to make this island our home and we have made a nice, comfortable lifestyle for ourselves through a lot of hard work. We have fresh meat in the form of a herd of goats. The same herd also supplies a small dairy and so we have fresh milk and cheese. There are plenty of fresh fruits and vegetables growing everywhere, some of which we tend and farm properly to ensure ongoing crops. We also have a small fish farm in one of the bays close to where we all live. We have a generator farm which supplies power to all of our houses and we have secured enough fuel in tankers to keep our generators and vehicles going for many generations. There are canned and dried goods aplenty in various warehouses and supermarkets all over the island, so we are pretty much set up here. All in all, we have a good lifestyle. The introduction of another seventeen people in the shape of your good selves is not really going to put any strain on our resources. We have held a meeting between the existing residents of the island and have decided that, subject to a trial period where we can all meet and integrate a few times on neutral ground, that it will be okay for you all to settle here on the island with us and we can all form one large community – kind of 'safety in numbers'. You are all aware of the 'incident' between the lads here", Carl gestured towards Joe Muhler, Wako Tamotei, Gareth Crook, Jim Wyles and Jim Parkin. "Well we believe that everyone deserves a second chance, especially given the situation that we all find ourselves in. So, after a few meetings between the groups, if everything goes well and everyone hits it off, we'll start the process of finding you all homes on the island".

Joe Muhler stood up and, in reply said, "That's great news Carl and once again on behalf of me and the four lads here, we apologise profusely for the events in Australia and to show how serious we are….", he nodded towards the other four submariners, who disappeared below decks for a few seconds and came back with a few weapons and magazines of ammunition……"pleased to hand over to you all of our weapons. We only brought them with us in case there was any trouble on our voyage here but you can have them now. I'm sure we will no longer need them".

Next, the large frame of the doctor, Matt Payne took to the stage as he stood up and cleared his throat. The chatter that had developed quietened down and he spoke. "On behalf of all of us here I'd like to thank you guys", he nodded towards Carl, Wayne and Josh. "Speaking from experience and months on a boat with them, I can assure you that these five lads", he pointed to the five submariners, "have been a great help to the rest of us. They told us about the trouble back in Australia. They told us all about your group, and they have been instrumental in looking after us, organising this voyage and getting us all here safely. Whatever they mat have been or done in the past is behind them now and I applaud you for giving them and us a chance to be part of your community. Our small group here has many skills between us, which will become apparent in due course, and will be of great benefit to a small community such as I am sure we are going to become. I'd like to propose a toast. Everyone raise your glasses."

The twenty people on board the magnificent vessel all raised their glasses in unison. "To all of us", toasted Matt, "*The Survivors*".

"The survivors" everyone shouted, taking a sip from their drinks, followed by lots of excited chatter as people turned towards their friends and started small group discussions. Matt Payne and Joe Muhler motioned to Carl, Wayne, Josh and the beautiful Leslie Dorfman - who Wayne could not take his eyes off – to join them for a chat down below in the main salon of the cruiser.

They all went down the fantastically varnished, dark teak stairwell into a huge, ornate room that wouldn't have looked amiss in a mansion. There were sofas of pure white leather; bookcases teaming with leather bound books and a very chic, polished mahogany bar with half a dozen barstools around it. Behind the bar was a very impressive selection of spirits on optic and glass fronted fridges containing a huge selection of beers, soft drinks and wines. Carl noted to himself that the place was extremely well looked after considering the long voyage the vessel had just undertaken and thought that this bode well and showed the influence that the 'university set' must have had on the submariners.

The small group of six settled themselves on barstools after Joe Muhler had poured them all a drink of their choice. After some initial small talk, Leslie took up the narrative. "I don't know how much you know about what has happened to the planet", she began, "but I can give you a professional guess. That's all it will be but I am basing the guess on my professional knowledge and training in Astral Physics and Astronomy".

Carl, Wayne and Josh all indicated that they would indeed like to hear what she had to theorise on the subject.

She took a deep breath and began again. "Well we all know that many months ago some form of astral body collided with our moon. This meteor, or small planet or whatever it was must have been travelling at speeds only barely imaginable to us and must have been on a trajectory that was shielded from our major earth telescopes by it's positioning in alignment with the moon. These points I assume, because none of the major tracking stations anywhere in the world had any knowledge of, or gave any warning of what was about to happen. When the collision took place, it was of such magnitude that it seems to have completely destroyed our moon. I'm also assuming that the collision gave off some kind of radiated frequency, once again completely unknown to us on this planet with our limited grasp of astral sciences, which managed to permeate and destroy all living tissue unless that tissue was protected by either water or earth down to a depth of a few metres – not sure how deep, but the fact that we are all still here bears testimony to this theory. For weeks after the collision I observed the skies at night with the telescope at the Astronomy department at the University of Sydney". She took a slight pause, sipped her gin and tonic, took a deep breath and started again.

"I noticed that there was a huge amount of shooting star activity but different to anything I'd ever seen before – a lot closer to the earth's surface. It was in fact the debris of the moon and whatever it was that had collided into it, falling to earth. Most of it was in such small pieces that it burned up and destroyed itself on entry into the earth's atmosphere as it was caught by our gravity. I'm sure bigger fragments must have landed in some places on earth but I would not imagine that they would be large enough to cause any major damage. More worrying is what I discovered next. Thinking about the implications of rays or frequencies that could destroy living tissue, I started to worry about radiation and fall-out. I decided to take atmospheric readings with a Geiger Counter and......I'm sure you can all guess what's coming next.......yep, we have all been exposed to quite high levels of radiation, even though we were shielded from the initial blast. The radiation we have picked up is from the fall-out; the particles that have been drifting down into our atmosphere since the day of the collision".

Joe and Matt obviously had heard these theories before but there was a stunned silence for a few seconds before Carl interrupted and asked, "So, what exactly are we talking about here? How high are the levels that we have been exposed to and what can we expect as a result of this exposure?"

Leslie replied, "Ah well that goes beyond my level of expertise I'm afraid but the good doctor here has a reasonable idea of what we can expect.....over to you Matt".

Matt Payne stood up, walked behind the bar, poured himself another double shot of Jack Daniels and carried on the conversation as he walked back and took up position once again on his barstool. Carl, Wayne and Josh were riveted by the conversation and watched him avidly as he re-seated himself.

"Again, this is not really my area of expertise" he began. "My background is a military one and my primary skills, as well as being a GP, are in treating trauma wounds such as those sustained in battlefield conditions. But since Leslie reported her findings to me I have done some research on the subject of radiation poisoning and the subsequent illnesses that can be characteristic depending on the levels and duration of exposure. Based on Leslie's Geiger counter readings none of us are in any immediate or imminent danger. In fact some of us may die a natural death from other illnesses or diseases before the effects of our radiation poisoning manifests itself. However, eventually, manifest itself it will, and in our later years, those of us that haven't already succumbed to any of God's other 'surprises' can expect to die of cancer of some kind – almost guaranteed – but, on a more cheerful note, I reckon it could take anything up to 15 years or more for any symptoms to become apparent. I believe we are talking levels at a similar or slightly lesser lever to the Chernobyl incident in Russia back in the nineteen eighties or whenever it was".

There was another period of reflective silence and, before anyone else could say anything, Matt spoke again, an octave louder and in a bright, cheery tone, "Anyway, look on the bright side. I'm going to find the local hospital, set up a surgery and we'll have so much bloody morphine on our hands that no bugger will even know they're poorly, let alone care", he laughed.

The mood broke and the other five all laughed with him, even though the new news was a shock to Carl, Wayne and Josh.

The six left their barstools and headed back up on deck to join the rest of the boat's passengers. It was then decided that the day after tomorrow, the island's residents would host a huge beach party and barbecue on one of the island's nicest beaches. Festivities would start at noon and go on until….whenever….and it would give everyone a chance to mix and get to know each other. The beach was pointed out on the boat's charts by Wayne and the three friends then took their leave and headed back to their villas.

CHAPTER THIRTY FIVE

Two days later the beach party went ahead as scheduled. Leading up to it had been a lot of work for the islanders. They had rigged up a portable generator to power lights, a music system and fridges which were overflowing with wine, beer, champagne and soft drinks. Abe and Rube had even found a small Portaloo company that they had 'borrowed' two Portaloos from and set them up just off the beach in the dunes.

A giant gas powered barbecue with a spit rotisserie attachment had been set up and now bore a whole goat which had been butchered for the occasion. Chief barbecue chef – self appointed – was Mick Dwight, ably assisted by Dave Bullough. Both were already in an advanced state of inebriation but the smells emanating from the barbecue were fantastic. As well as the spit roasted goat, there were whole fish roasting over the gas flamed coals, along with oysters, mussels and scallops, courtesy of a recent diving trip by Carl and Mandy. Casual tables had been set up and were groaning under the weight of fruit, bread and salads set out upon them.

People were mingling and chatting; moving from group to group. Ex-publicans, Mike and Hannah had come into their own and were making sure everyone had drinks. They had even organised a load of beach games. Off to one side there was a makeshift volleyball court with the boundaries marked in the sand and a net made from two broom handles and a piece of rope. There was a game in progress with five a side and nearly every point was won or lost amid howls of laughter.

On another part of the beach there was an old fashioned 'mop race' in progress. This also was the focus of much hilarity as it was played in relay teams, with the idea being to chug a beer as fast as possible, run fifty metres to a point on the beach where there was a mop handle waiting for the competitor. They then had to place their forehead on the mop handle, with the other end on the floor and then spin themselves around ten times as fast as possible. Then, feeling light-headed from chugging the beer and dizzy from spinning, they had to try to sprint back to their team so that the next member could take his or her turn.

All in all, the beach party was a great success, as were the next couple of meetings between the two groups. The last meeting was at the island's bowling alley, where after a couple of days playing around with generators and exploring the internal systems, Klem and Tom had managed to get all the bowling lanes working. A great night was had by all and it was after this final meeting of the two groups that it was unanimously decided that it would be fine for the crew of the cruiser to settle on the island.

Over the next few weeks, relationships were formed and villas were sought out in the vicinity of the other villas. New cars, people carriers, 4 x 4s and even motorbikes arrived from all over the island, depending on people's tastes.

The small taverna at the top of the hill was taken over by the two Jims – Parkin and Wyles, and was cleaned up, restocked and over the next few weeks became the local village pub. The guys opened up every evening so that anyone could come and have a drink and a chinwag. Sometimes they had nobody in and other times there could be a dozen or more customers, although strictly speaking, they weren't customers, because all drinks were free.

Over the next few months, the community grew. Matt Payne, or as everyone was now calling him, The Doc, had raided the local hospital and had set up a miniature hospital and operating theatre in his huge villa, which had fantastic views over the Mediterranean. In fact, it was where all three of the community's newest arrivals were born, with Lucy, Helena and Hannah all having baby boys under the skilful watch of The Doc.

Wayne had flirted with Leslie Dorfman, finally plucking up courage to ask her out. After a brief courtship, she moved out of the small villa she had originally moved into on her own and they officially became a couple, both living in Wayne's villa. In fact there were a few little romances blossoming and over the months, the community settled down into a day to day routine.

People were appointed responsibilities to ensure that they had all they needed. Some were assigned to look after generators and fuel. Some were assigned to regular weekly trips to the island's cash and carry warehouses to resupply everyone with food, drink, cleaning materials and anything else they could lay their hands on to make life more comfortable. Some people were assigned to the dairy, some to the fish farm, and some to the goat herd. Helena and Lucy took it upon themselves to operate a daily crèche where little Manuela, baby Jessica and the three new arrivals could be deposited on a daily basis while the grown ups went about their daily tasks.

To supplement the fish farm, Carl and Mandy had taken it upon themselves to create a shellfish farm as well. Whilst diving they had come across areas of the coast that were rich in mussels, oysters, scallops and langoustine. Over a period of several weeks, they built escape proof pens down in the marina and began the long process of stocking the pens with as much shellfish as they could catch on each diving trip that they took.

It was after one such trip as they sat drinking chilled champagne back at the poolside of their villa, baby Jessica playing quietly on the lawn with her toys, Carl said to Mandy, "I know I've said it before and, in the light of the current worldwide dilemma that the human race finds itself in, it probably sounds crass; but for me this is *perfecto mundo*. No mortgage, no bills to pay, no money worries. If we go to work, it's because we choose to. I actually love this lifestyle".

Mandy concurred but expressed a small amount of concern by saying, "No it doesn't sound crass and I do agree with you but I do think that, if we are going to re-populate the whole planet eventually and ensure that our children have the necessary skills to do so, we are going to have to group into bigger communities. We need people with a more diverse range of skills and professions and we need teachers that can pass those skills on to the children that will inevitably come along over the next few years. I think we should give some thought to a long term plan with these things in mind. Short term, I agree with you; life is great. But I am thinking of what life will be like for Jessica when we are no longer here."

CHAPTER THIRTY SIX

About six months after the new arrivals had moved permanently onto the island, a meeting was called, discreetly, by Leslie Dorfman at the villa she and Wayne shared. They had asked only Carl and another member of the new arrivals, Jeremy Long who had been one of Leslie's colleagues on the staff at the university. He used to be head of the university meteorology department and was head lecturer in that subject as well as supplying data to several Australian TV and radio networks. Since he had arrived and settled on Crete, he had scoured the whole island for the instrumentation and paraphernalia of his trade in order that he could set up a small weather monitoring station to try and keep abreast of what was happening with the world's weather patterns since the phenomena occurred (some sixteen months ago now).

The four of them settled down in the leather sofas of the main lounge in Wayne and Leslie's house and Leslie started the conversation.

"As we all know it has been about sixteen months now since our moon was destroyed. We all had inkling that the world's weather patterns would be disrupted and altered to some extent but none of us at the time had a clue in what way these changes would manifest themselves. On our voyage here a few months ago, the five lads from the navy all commented on the strength of the winds and the lack of tidal currents. However they did say that, although there were significant differences from what they would normally have expected in the areas that we sailed through, there was nothing to cause immediate alarm. Now though, Jeremy has noticed some findings that may cause concern especially when coupled with some discoveries of my own."

Jeremy took over the conversation. "Well as you can imagine, my monitoring equipment is quite primitive but it was the best I could find on such a small island. However, a few anomalies have become apparent. Firstly, something all of you should have noticed but probably haven't because none of us lives our lives by the clock any more. The length of the average day has shortened quite considerably. What I mean by that is that from sunrise on day one to sunrise on day two is now no longer twenty four hours but has reduced to just below twenty three hours and has been decreasing slowly for some time now. What this means, and correct me if I'm wrong Leslie, is that because the earth's daily spin is no longer influenced by the gravity of the moon, this spin has speeded up. It now takes less than twenty three hours for the earth to do one complete 260 degree cycle and it looks like this period is decreasing by a few seconds per day. The other changes that I have noticed, having compared weather records for the island going back for the last fifty years or so, are these. Average wind speeds are up. Although never a hugely tidal sea, the Mediterranean did have a minimal tidal influence from the moon's gravity. However it is now completely tide less and the sea level has risen considerably. Average hours of sunshine appear to be decreasing slightly, obviously due to the earth's increased spin and average temperatures are up slightly as well."

Leslie continued, "None of these findings, at this stage, are great cause for concern – although Jeremy will continue to monitor things".

"Yes", he interjected, "and I would like to take a couple of field trips out to other places, perhaps in a light aircraft, just to have a look at a few other things. I'd like to know if the permanent snow is melting on some of the highest Alps peaks for example. I'd like to see if there are visible changes in the levels of rivers and large lakes. Perhaps see if there is any change in activity on a couple of volcanoes such as Etna. We could also check on the tidal activity on one of the Atlantic coasts because I feel pretty confident that all tidal activity will have ceased by now".

Carl agreed that this was a good idea and volunteered his services as a pilot.

Leslie continued. "Now, even more worrying than Jeremy's news is my latest findings. As you all know I observe the skies at night with a very powerful telescope I found in the island's observatory. Everything seems as normal up there as far as I can see with the exception of one discovery. We appear to have a new star that has appeared in the night skies. When I first started to observe it was barely discernable but as the months have gone on it is growing in size. It has a slightly orange tint to it as well and it is visible to the human eye now. This is worrying because stars do no, as a rule, grow in size. This leads me to the conclusion that it may not actually be a new star but rather a very large meteor or another smaller planet which has somehow been nudged or dislodged and is now moving at some speed through space. Unfortunately, because it is growing in size when looked at from our perspective; this would indicate that it is heading in our general direction. Now this is nothing to worry about at this stage, because even if it is heading in our general direction, a one degree shift in trajectory would mean that it sails harmlessly past us, missing earth by millions of miles and no-one on the surface of the planet being any the wiser. I'm just bringing it to your attention because I think it is something that we should monitor. I also don't want us to let any of the others know any of these findings because we don't want to start a panic. Do we all agree?"

Jeremy, Carl and Wayne all nodded their assent and Carl said, "Perhaps we should meet up once a month and have a chat just like this to be appraised of how things are changing? Meanwhile, Jeremy and I will plan a field trip and bring back some meteorological findings from other areas that may give us a clearer global picture of weather change, water levels, tides, winds and temperatures".

They all agreed and Jeremy and Wayne decided they would head straight off and start planning their trip. "No time like the present eh?" asked Jeremy.

CHAPTER THIRTY SEVEN

Two days later they had their itinerary planned. They would fly initially east over the island of Sicily where they could check out if recent events had had a bearing on the threat posed by volcanoes that were still active. They would fly over Etna and see what kind of activity, if any was going on. Theoretically there should just be a few tendrils of smoke as the volcano had not even had a minor eruption for many years now.
They would then fly north across the southern European Alps in France and Switzerland to check out the highest peaks that would normally have snow deposits on them all year around.
They would then stop, rest and re-fuel somewhere in the southern regions of France, perhaps Nice, and then, the following day carry on west through France, Spain and up through Portugal to follow the Atlantic coastline up to the North of France. They would then land somewhere that would really be affected by the slightest change in tidal activity; somewhere on the coastline of the English Channel, probably Brighton. Here they would stay for a twenty four hour period to give them enough time to accurately measure tidal movement and make comparisons to how those same tides would have behaved this time of year before the phenomena struck.
Day three would see them headed back to Crete, having refuelled at Brighton airport. The doc asked for permission to accompany them to see if he could salvage any medicines or medical equipment that was not available at the small hospital on the island. He also wanted to pick up a few important text books, in English, which may come in useful in future should he be called upon to perform any tricky operations or emergency surgery. The three of them set off on a bright, Mediterranean morning, waved off by a few of the gang who had accompanied them to the airport to help with fuelling and checking the aircraft. They had with them a huge list of items that other members of the group had requested they bring back if they could find them. These were primarily food items that people had a craving for, such as 'proper crisps, proper chocolate and proper beer'.

While they were gone, life continued as normal. The children played in the crèche, the chores were completed; the taverna remained an evening focal point for, social drinking, speculative conversations about what the future might hold and the odd game of cards, pool and darts.
Leslie also continued religiously to monitor the night skies. Secretly she was quite alarmed about the steady growth in size of the new 'star' that seemed to be heading in their direction. It was not yet close enough to discern exactly what kind of celestial body it was but she could notice every evening a minute increase in the size of the entity. Although at this stage she had no idea of its speed or the possible timescale of its passing close to, or, God forbid, colliding with earth, she was genuinely worried.

During this period, while everyone waited for the return of the weather scouting party, one of the newcomers, made a wonderful discovery. Twenty two year old Alice Gordon had been a student of veterinary sciences at the University of Sydney. Originally from

Sydney, now living in total, blissful sin with Josh Cransley, she had been out for a stroll along the banks of a small stream some miles inland where she had driven as an escape and to get a bit of exercise. As she strolled along the bank of the stream, the sides steepened in one area and formed quite high sandbanks. These sandbanks were dotted with small holes; "sand martins' nests", she thought to herself as she continued along, suddenly stopping dead in her tracks. In front of her, flying around without a care in the world and darting into and out of the small holes were in fact actual, live sand martins. She knew from her ornithological studies that sand martins nested several metres deep into the sandbanks, putting their nests and eggs out of reach of most of their natural predators. This had obviously protected a few brooding hens that had been incubating nests full of eggs at the time of the phenomena. It was the only explanation for what she was now seeing.

She then turned her mind to other species that could have survived in different areas of the world. Bats, obviously; lots of different species of insects, reptiles, rabbits, hares; in fact the more she thought about it the more excited she became. The cause of her excitement, as well as the discovery of another life form as a scientific fact, was the potential that she had just realised for future food supplies for the group.

If they could scour the island she was sure that hey would be able to find, somewhere, a colony of rabbits. She was sure some of these could be captured alive and used as the basis for a rabbit farm and a constant source of protein for the group.

She wasn't even sure if colony was the correct word for a grouping of rabbits, but she didn't care because she was even more excited about the other realisation that had dawned on her.

She tried to recall the lectures at University relating to this subject. Diapause was the term for the subject. Diapause is a genetic switch that results in suspended animation in which embryonic cell growth and development are reversibly stopped or slowed.

Diapause occurs in a diverse range of vertebrates and invertebrates that includes insects, copepods (crustaceans), fish, birds, rodents, and marsupials (animals with pouches, such as the kangaroo) and other mammals, including deer.

In chicken eggs, development stops whenever the hen gets off the egg and the eggs cool down and starts back again when the hen returns to her nest. This is considered a temperature-dependent diapause.

"Chickens", she thought to herself. "Chickens' eggs can lie dormant for months if they're not incubated and then be hatched out many months later once the hen decides she has a clutch of a size worth incubating. The island must have a chicken farm somewhere for the supply of eggs and the supply of chickens. There's an outside chance that there will be a stash of eggs somewhere that was untouched by the flare. Perhaps stored in a cellar somewhere......I'm sure I can find and incubator somewhere.....". Her thoughts trailed off and she turned back to re-trace her steps back to where she had left her Porsche Boxster. "Funny how many of us drive Porsches these days", she smiled to herself as she climbed into the open top sports car and, excitedly speeded back to the villa to share her potentially brilliant ideas with Josh and the rest of the community. "The rabbits will be easy, I'm sure", she thought. "Not too sure about the chicken eggs though. Not sure what kind of shelf life they have during which they can still be successfully incubated".

She pulled up outside her villa with a screech of brakes and dashed inside to share her findings with Josh.

They decided not to share her findings with the others in case their searched for both rabbits and chicken eggs proved fruitless. Instead, they devoted the next two days to scouring the island for both. On their first day, armed with small nets operated by slip knots which Josh had fashioned from old bits of fish netting from the old fishing boats near the marina, they successfully located a small hillock teeming with rabbits. "How come we never thought of this earlier or even spotted them before", thought Josh to himself as he set about placing his nets over each and every hole leading into the warren. There were nineteen of them dotted all over the hillock, which sat in the middle of an old outdoor go-karting track. Josh made a mental note to return here with the guys and see if they could get some of the karts working. That would make for some fun days out. They finished laying the nets, each one staked down by a small tent peg. If a rabbit ran into one, it would close around the small animal, trapping it without injuring or killing it. They decided they would leave the nets and return in twenty four hours to see how much success they had had.

Alice and Josh had done a little homework on the chicken and egg subject. They had scoured local telephone directories for the island and had found five entries for chicken breeders or egg producers. Armed with the addresses and a couple of maps of the island they set out to see what they could find.

The first two were little more than smallholdings with no signs of life whatsoever. There had obviously been chickens here at one stage but the businesses must have been very small, probably only just sustaining the families that ran them.

The third site was different. They drove into a large concreted courtyard through large wrought iron gates. The sign over the gates proclaimed *J. Macarios – Poultry Breeder* and Alice got a little flutter of excitement in her stomach as they drove through the gates. There were large, slatted wood poultry sheds, capable of housing hundreds of birds and a series of smaller outbuildings as well as a main farmhouse.

Searches of all the buildings revealed nothing which was disappointing and, Alice thought to herself, also a bit strange, because they had not discovered any incubation areas. These storage buildings were obviously for the chicks once they were hatched but there was no hatchery area.

They were about to leave, despondently, when Josh suggested that they have a look inside the farmhouse itself. The large, whitewashed building stood off to the side of the main yard and was very pretty in that authentic Greek kind of ramshackle way. As they went in there was a musty smell. There was a thick covering of dust on everything but apart from that it looked as if the family had just popped out for the day. There were plates still on the table and in the sink, jackets hanging over the backs of chairs and jars of honey and jams on the table.

A search of the house revealed nothing remarkable until Josh discovered a large door leading off from the scullery area. It led down to a cellar. Josh popped back to the car and came back armed with two flashlights and they went down into the cellar together. As they reached the bottom few steps they could see that it was like a Tardis. There was a main corridor and several large rooms leading off from it in a labyrinth of passageways. Each room had an air conditioning unit attached to the wall and several of the rooms had been decked out as large incubation chambers. They had struck gold. The cellar was the perfect place to hatch out the eggs because of the protection from the extremes of heat in the summer, hence the air conditioning. Other rooms were done out as holding pens, obviously for the chicks in the first few days of life before they were transferred to the larger rearing buildings in the courtyard. The pens were now just filled with straw and debris, which was probably all that remained of the unfortunate chicks that were left down here to die a horrible death of starvation and dehydration, having – unknowingly - survived one of the world's worst ever natural disasters.

The incubation rooms were a different story however. There were several large incubators all full of eggs or of the remains of tiny chicks. Alice doubted if any of these were viable because of the stages of incubation they would have been at by the time the poser failed. However, in all of the incubation rooms, there were boxes and boxes of carefully stacked and packaged eggs, which Alice assumed were all fertilised eggs awaiting their turn to be put through the incubators.

She and Josh did several trips back to the car with boxes of eggs and with two medium size incubators which had a 48 egg capacity with automatic egg turning facility. Egg turning during incubation is vital to the viability of hatching eggs and it was something that, in the wild, all brooding hens of all bird species performed as a natural instinct.

Once back home they quickly converted the garage into a makeshift hatchery and, as Alice carefully loaded the incubators with eggs, she explained in detail to Josh, the process in the natural word of Diapause, adding her reservations about the timescale since these eggs were fertilised.

"Something about two and a half times the lifespan of the animal in question, springs to mind for egg viability after fertilisation, but don't quote me on it. We'll find out soon enough in twenty one to twenty five days", she said to Josh.

After breakfast the next day, still without mentioning their plans to anyone else in the community, they drove back out to the go-karting track in the huge Toyota 4 x 4 pick up truck that they used as their utility back up vehicle. They were going to check on the success of their rabbit hunting expedition. They were overjoyed as they approached the mound that housed the warren. Nearly every net had an animal in it, and after a couple of escapees and one very nasty nip on the wrist sustained by Josh from a particularly lively character, they counted nine rabbits as they bundled them out of the nets and packed them into cardboard boxes that they had brought with them for the purpose of transporting the animals. They also re-set the nets one more time and decided to check back tomorrow for a second batch of the animals.

On the drive back home they stopped at a big agricultural warehouse they had spotted on their travels and loaded up with fence posts, chicken wire, food and water hoppers and hutches that would serve inside a purpose built compound as sleeping quarters for the colony (Alice still wasn't sure if that was the correct word. "Must look it up", she thought).

CHAPTER THIRTY EIGHT

It was around this time when Carl started having the dreams. At first they were quite vague but as the nights wore on they became more and more vivid, almost as if they were real. When he awoke each morning he could have sworn that he had lived through the experience. One morning he decided he would tell Mandy about the dreams. They were sat outside by the swimming pool on a beautiful sunny morning sipping freshly squeezed orange juice made from the plentiful supplies of oranges picked every week from the

surrounding groves. As he sliced off a chunk of watermelon for his breakfast he said to
Mandy, "I've been having some very strange dreams just lately you know– almost
lifelike".

"Oh really", replied Mandy casually. "What about?"

"Well they're strange – very strange. Everyone from the group is in them. The whole
world is filled with brilliant light, almost too bright to be able to open your eyes, yet I can
see perfectly well. It all takes place as if it's in slow motion. The whole group is heading
towards a certain point from various directions. I don't know exactly where it is but I
vaguely recognise the place. It gets a little clearer each night, and when we arrive
together we all stand in a circle and hold hands. But, at the same time as I am dreaming
this I also see other groups similar to ours in different parts of the world and they are all
doing the same thing as us. The light gets more and more intense until I can no longer
keep my eyes open and it's at that point that I wake up every time".

"Oh my god", exclaimed Mandy. "I have exactly the same dream every night. I mean –
exactly the same. I was going to mention it to you but I was afraid you would think I was
mad. What do you think it means? I wonder if anyone else is having the same dream."

"Well we can find out if the others are having the same dream. I bet it's got something to
do with the bright light that is approaching the planet you know. Something to do with
waves or frequencies beyond our comprehension. Come on, finish your breakfast and
we'll go and have a word with Leslie. She may have a clue as to what is going on".

They walked around to the villa that Leslie now shared with Wayne. Leslie was sat in the
garden reading a book when they shouted "Hello" together. Leslie explained that Wayne
was down at the marina with his fishing gear.

They all moved indoors and sat around the table in the kitchen. Leslie opened an ice cold
bottle of Chablis, even though it was only just after eleven in the morning, qualifying it
by saying, "Well – every day seems like a holiday to me now. Life is so different to
before….you know….the occurrence; and I have to be honest with you – I like it. I don't
miss all the people, the bills, the mortgage, the daily grind of working to exist. I prefer
life now to life then".

"I'm with you there", agreed Carl as he took a sip of wine. He then retold his dreams to
Leslie and explained that Mandy had been having similar dreams. Leslie listened with her
jaw hanging open in disbelief and interjected excitedly before Carl could finish.

"Wayne and I have been having the same dreams" she announced. It must definitely have
something to do with this sphere of immense light that is heading towards us. It's the
only thing that is common to all of us and there is so much that is unknown about
radiation and frequencies and how they can affect the workings of the human mind. I will
bet that all the others are having similar dreams but I don't really know if I can offer a
scientific explanation if that is the case. Even though I am a scientific person, my mind is
more open to something a bit more celestial or supernatural about this situation. I have
been observing the sphere every night through my telescope as it gets nearer and nearer
and I find it strangely comforting. Really, I should be panicking wildly in case it is
similar to what wiped out the rest of humanity last time; but instead, every time I observe
it I am filled with a sort of inner peace. I have a foreboding that something is going to
happen concerning the light but it's not a bad feeling. I also get the same good feeling
about the dreams…as if….well, if there is a God of some sort it's as if he has a plan for

us all and the approach of this light signals the beginning of that plan being put into action".

They agreed that they would split up and go wandering around the rest of the villas and the taverna and talk to the other members of the group to ascertain if anyone else had been having the dreams. They would meet up back here at Lesley and Wayne's house tonight for a barbecue and invite everyone along that they could meet up with and chat to throughout the day. Carl volunteered to walk down to the Marina to see Wayne and said that the pair of them would stop at the Taverna on their way back.

The two girls split the rest of the houses up between them and off they went to question the rest of the group of friends.

CHAPTER THIRTY NINE

Around seven thirty that evening every single man, woman and child in the group was present at Wayne and Lesley's poolside and there was a huge buzz of excitement in the air as well as the thick smoke and strong aromas of grilling goat meat, rabbit and seafood from the charcoal barbecue.

It transpired that everyone in the group, even little Manuela, had been having similar dreams. Some not as clear as others and some with slightly differing aspects but basically the same dream was being shared by each and every one of them.

They were stood around in small groups chatting excitedly between themselves, speculating as to what it could all mean. The brightness of the new sphere was very prominent in the clear, star studded sky and was even bigger now than the moon used to be and even brighter. On evenings when there was no cloud in the sky it almost seemed as light as an early summer morning at dusk.

Speculation was rife in each of the small conversational groups as to what the dreams could mean. Did it mean that there were definitely other groups similar to themselves in other parts of the world? Was the new sphere of light going to have a significant impact on earth in some way as it got closer and closer? Would it destroy them? Did the dreams mean it was going to be the end? No-one knew but everyone had an opinion of some sort, however, surprisingly enough, everyone was buoyant about it. Nobody seemed to be afraid that it could indeed signal the end of things for them. It was as if the beams from the sphere had infected them all with a 'feel good' factor and no-one felt anything other than that the sphere was good news for them all. There was no fact to base this on, only a general feeling among themselves; but a very strong feeling.

The night went well. Everyone got a bit tipsy. Alice admitted that she had had no success with her egg incubation experiments and declared either that the eggs had been inert for too long a period to be successfully incubated, or, they had also been destroyed by the initial 'occurrence' and would never hatch.

As the evening wound down and everyone tottered off to bed they agreed that they would get together again every week and compare notes on how the dreams were going for each of them.

CHAPTER FORTY

The weeks rolled on through autumn of that year and into the pleasant, sun filled Mediterranean winter so typical to the Greek Islands. The sphere moved ever closer to earth until, by early December it almost filled the sky and there was no difference any more between day and night. It was obvious now to everyone that the sphere of light was there as an indication and precursor of something huge that was about to happen. Yet everyone still felt that same overwhelming feeling of peacefulness and tranquillity about the situation; almost as if the rays from the sphere were infecting them all with some kind of tranquilising drug.

Everyone was having the dreams now – but exactly identical – down to the last detail. Everyone from the group is still in the dreams. The whole world is still filled with the beautiful, brilliant light. Except now it has become clear that the whole group is heading towards a field at the rear of the villas; the field where they currently keep the herd of goats. Everyone still stands in a circle and holds hands. However, now everyone is dreaming of a date; and that date is Christmas day – the twenty-fifth of December. Everyone also is dreaming of other groups of survivors meeting up in a similar fashion in different places all over the world, all doing the same thing – standing in a circle, holding hands on Christmas day and looking into the light, which now seems to have become so bright and all-consuming that it appears to have taken over everything. Once again though, it is at this point that everyone wakes up from the dream. Even to the slowest members of the group it was becoming apparent that something totally out of their control and beyond their comprehension as mere humans was going to unfold in a couple of weeks time on the twenty-fifth.

Over the next few days leading up that date the group started to meet for a social event of some kind every evening. It was almost as if there was a feeling of safety in numbers. Nearly everyone had a turn at hosting an evening, either a barbecue or a paella evening or a dinner party. The lads even had a games evening down in the taverna with competitions in cards, dominoes, pool and darts. There was very little spoken any more between them about the dreams. There seemed little point. What was about to happen was totally out of their control and would happen anyway regardless of how much they discussed it or mused over it.

It was decided that Mandy and Carl would host a grand Christmas party on the twenty-fourth - Christmas Eve - and everyone would stay over and see in Christmas day and the sunrise, followed by breakfast and an opening of presents.
Mandy had seen a cross section of these presents and thought secretly to herself that Christmas day would be a long one. She had seen everything hidden away – from Porsches to luxury yachts. It all seemed a bit pointless really because money was no object and any one of them could virtually have anything they wanted anyway. However it was tradition and it would be fun.

CHAPTER FORTY ONE

Everyone turned up at Carl and Mandy's house around lunchtime on Christmas Eve. Carl and some of the boys had been busy and had built a huge cooking pit complete with a huge roasting spit on which spun two butchered kids. The handle was being turned by different beer swilling members of the male fraternity, swapping on a regular basis due to the huge amount of heat being emitted by the charcoals. The smells emanating from it were mouth watering and there were regular visits to the spit from other group members to chat to the spit turner or to bring over a fresh bottle of ice cold beer for him.

Small groups were scattered around the swimming pool, chatting and laughing in the warm winter sun; Manuela was playing with the babies on the lawn. The immense, now almost godly light from the sphere seemed to permeate everything. It was strange how it could be so bright and yet everyone could see perfectly well. Also, it appeared not to give off any heat – only the brilliant light. It was surreal yet everyone seemed oblivious by now to it and daily life had just carried on around it.

The day was a roaring success. Mike Dwight had found a Father Christmas suit in one of the town shops and posed a comical figure in it issuing forth great guffaws of 'Ho Ho Ho' every so often.

Jo Muhler and Wako Timotei had embarked on a drinking contest earlier on in the afternoon and one was asleep on a sun lounger by the pool and the other had been put unceremoniously to bed in one of the spare rooms. Hardly surprising really, as they had polished off a full bottle of Vodka and a bottle of Baileys Irish Cream as well as an undetermined amount of beer!

Midnight approached and everyone was still in good spirits. The light from the sphere suddenly increased unexpectedly to a brilliance that was beyond comprehension. It was accompanied by a low, deep humming sound that seemed to permeate everything and to vibrate things with a resonance that was almost painful on the eardrums and seemed to vibrate the very core of the soul.

Jo and Wako both woke up immediately and made their way trance like to the other group members.

Something had happened to everyone. There was no more chatter. Everyone was silent with an intense look on their faces. Mothers gathered up babies in their arms. Lucy grabbed hold of Manuela's hand and everyone started making their way across the back of the garden towards the field at the rear. No-one said a word to anyone else. There was no need. They were all acting as one single entity, mesmerized by whatever strange unearthly sounds, light and rays were being emitted and absorbed by their bodies. They were all in a trance and did not even acknowledge each other as they negotiated the fence into the field and began to form into a circle, just as they had been doing in their dreams for months. They were powerless to do anything else. Something had taken hold of their minds and their bodies now – something not of this world and something incomprehensible to them was now conducting their movements and their thoughts on their behalf.

Eventually everyone was in the field and the circle had been formed, just as it had in the dreams. They were all holding hands and, as a single body, they all simultaneously turned their heads upwards to look into the brilliance of the light. As they did so, the light grew impossibly brighter, swamping them, blotting them out completely. Everyone's mind was as one and each of them was aware of being a part of everything, part of everyone still left on the planet, part of the earth, part of every plant and creature – everything everywhere on earth was as one.

Then – there was nothing........................

CHAPTER FORTY TWO

The man awoke. He was naked and had been laid on the damp, dew-dropped morning grass. He was not aware of his nakedness. He was in an orchard. He was hungry but he knew he must not eat the fruit from the trees that surrounded him. He had an amazing feeling of Déjà vu.

Maybe this time things would be different..................

THE END